# BAD GUY LAWYER

# CHUCK MARTEN

# BAD GUY LAWYER

Down & Out Books
3959 Van Dyke Road, Suite 265
Lutz, FL 33558
DownAndOutBooks.com

Cover design by Zach McCain

ISBN: 1-64396-249-3
ISBN-13: 978-1-64396-249-8

*To Logan*

# CHAPTER 1—September 28, 1987

"Hi, I'm Brandi. You wanna dance?"

That's what she said. What she meant was, *Do you want* a *dance?* As opposed to, *Do you want* to *dance?* This was not the kind of place where men and women danced together.

The only thing Guy McCann wanted was to sit alone at the bar and enjoy his Macallan eighteen-year, neat. But it was early on a Monday night and the working girls outnumbered the patrons. Guy felt like a piece of carrion being circled by a flock of body-lotion-and-glitter-covered vultures.

He tried to be polite. "No thanks," he said, offering up a half smile. "Maybe later."

"But I'm leaving soon." Her tone was that of a three-year-old asking to stay up another five minutes. "I might not be here later."

"Sorry," Guy said. "I've got my drink."

"Bring your drink." She offered up a coquettish smile.

"No, really. I'm okay."

"I can make you *better*." As she confidently delivered this guarantee, Brandi squeezed her upper arms together in a well-practiced maneuver that not-so-subtly lifted her cleavage closer to Guy's line of sight.

He paused. "That's very clever, but I'm not here for that." He glanced down at the silicone-filled orbs occupying her tube

1

top. "Or those." Her smile disappeared. "I'm just here to meet a friend. Until he shows up, I just want to drink my drink and not take up any more of your time, so..." The way he trailed off implied she should do likewise.

"Oh, I see," she said. "My mistake. I didn't realize you were a *tourist*."

His ears perked up. "I'm sorry?" he asked. "A what?"

"A tourist. Now that you've seen what boobies look like, I guess you can skip on back to the Blue Oyster Bar and tell your buddies all about it."

"Wait? What?" Then he got it. "Oh, I get it. Because I don't want a dance from you, I must be..." He put down his drink. "Okay, how much is it a dance?" Guy asked. "Five, right? Five bucks a song?"

He pulled out his wallet and produced a portrait of Abraham Lincoln, flattening it out on the bar in front of him.

"Here you go." Guy gestured to the legal tender on the counter. "It's for you. But I don't want you to dance. I just want you to sit here, at the bar, next to me, for a whole song. And during that song, I want you to keep completely silent. I don't want you to say a word. Just...sit there."

She looked at the sixteenth president of the United States. "Just to sit here?"

"In silence."

She shrugged. "Okay."

"Great," Guy said. "Then it's settled. I remind you that if you utter a single syllable, you will be in breach of contract, forfeiting any claim to our agreed-upon payment."

She eyed him queerly as she sank into the barstool next to him.

"I, however, have made no such agreement to remain silent. So I will exercise my option to speak freely."

Guy paused to take a sip from his drink. The DJ's amplified voice echoed harshly throughout the mostly empty clubroom as he announced that Shanna was arriving on the main stage. The music blasting from the house speakers segued from Santana's "Black Magic Woman" to Vanity's "Nasty Girl."

"Okay," Guy began, "I don't know what you see when you look in the mirror. But trust me, there is nothing here," he motioned to her face and torso in that order, "that is so compelling as to render it impossible for a heterosexual male of sound mind and body to decline the opportunity to pay you five dollars to dry hump him in front of the dozen or so drunken yokels that constitute the Monday night crowd in this dump. In fact, that you are stuck working the Monday night shift, in and of itself, should tell you something of your overall desirability, or lack thereof, to the opposite sex."

Her face hardened and she opened her mouth to retort. Guy cut her off by holding up his index finger
and glancing at the cash on the bar. She regained her composure, sat back into her barstool, and slowly crossed her right leg over her left.

"You should really consider the possibility that if I would rather sit by myself and drink my scotch than have you rub your surgically augmented tits in my face, it's an indictment of you, not of me," Guy continued. "Although to be fair, this scotch is pretty damn good."

He paused to take another sip and placed the glass back on the bar.

"Do you actually know why it is men come here?" Guy cocked his head to the side. "No? Then I'll spell it out for you. It's to escape reality. To experience a fantasy. And you know what my fantasy is? It's a woman who's smart enough to realize that if I'm not interested in what I can see from across the room, then her slithering over here and shoving it in my face isn't going to help."

She was clenching her jaw so tightly her facial muscles were twitching.

"It used to be that a guy could come to a place like this and be left alone. You know, to enjoy the scenery without suffering that tired Betty-Boop-on-Spanish-Fly routine of yours. But you girls have gotten so goddamn pushy that it feels more like I'm in a used car lot than a goddamn titty bar. I just wanted to have a drink. That's why I'm sitting here. At the bar. If I wanted a dance, I'd be sitting over there. With the guys getting dances."

She wasn't even looking at him anymore. She just stared stiffly at the five-dollar bill on the bar. Her right leg was bouncing so forcefully that the surface of his scotch was resonating in concentric circles.

"So, in summary, once this song ends, please leave me and my scotch alone. Be certain, the only thing I want from your body is to see it from behind, getting smaller and smaller, as you walk farther and farther away from me."

And with that, the DJ asked everyone to give it up for Shanna. The six or seven regulars managed to muster up a forced applause as "Nasty Girl" transitioned into Madonna's "Lucky Star."

The song over, Brandi immediately grabbed the five. "You're an asshole," she growled, choking the bill with her fist as she disappeared back into the dark, smoke-filled abyss.

"Duly noted," Guy mumbled. He swiveled back to the bar, only to find that he had already finished his drink. Talking too much always seemed to go hand in hand with drinking too much. And vice versa.

He gestured for the bartender's attention, but before he could order another scotch, a large, broad-shouldered oaf sporting a Freddie Mercury mustache and a well-worn Stetson appeared and placed a hand on Guy's shoulder.

"Sorry, I'm late," Shady Mike said. Then to the bartender, "No, he's done. I'll take care of the tab."

Before Guy could protest, Shady Mike was pulling him to his feet. "He's in the back."

Guy wrestled himself free of Shady Mike's grip and craned his neck up at his tardy companion. Shady Mike had the build of a first-string offensive guard and the acumen of a third-string elephant shit shoveler, and for both reasons Guy tended to forgive his congenital lack of delicacy.

"He kept me waiting long enough." Guy straightened the front of his collared shirt and ran his fingers through his hair.

"Well, what do you want me to say? This isn't a German train station he's running here. Come on."

"Leave it open," Guy ordered the bartender. He turned and followed his companion away from the bar. Shady Mike led him toward the back of the club, past the men's room, down a dark hallway.

"Now remember," Shady Mike said. "You help Rico out, he's gonna help you. So try to show him some respect."

"Show respect to Rico the Pimp? You mean, like, curtsy when I enter?"

Shady Mike shook his head. "I mean, like, stop referring to him as Rico the Pimp."

"You know, titles are bestowed as a sign of honor."

"Maybe just try to talk as little as possible."

Guy shut his mouth and the two continued in silence. Lacking conversation to distract him, Guy realized how tense he was. He took a deep breath and tried to loosen his shoulders.

"Why do we always have to meet in places like this, anyway?"

Shady Mike raised an eyebrow. "Don't be such a tourist."

"I didn't even know that was an expression..." Guy was cut off by their arrival at a doorway guarded by a large, sullen bouncer. The bouncer glared down at Guy, who turned to Shady Mike, who rolled his eyes.

"Give me a break, Stewie," he said. "I was just here five minutes ago."

The bouncer opened the door and Guy followed Shady Mike into the small office, where the proprietor of the establishment was sitting behind a heavily dented steel typewriting desk. His beefy frame spilled out of a faded wife beater, and he studied Guy with an eerie curiosity, like he was deciding whether to eat him.

"You the *abogado?*" he asked.

"*Tal vez*," Guy replied. "You Rico the Pimp?"

Shady Mike winced.

Rico grinned at Guy. "Let's not stand on ceremony. Just Rico is fine." He motioned for Guy to take the chair sitting across from him. "I heard you know a couple things about getting guys out of a jam."

Guy started to feel comfortable. Not exactly in his element, but close to it. "Why don't you tell me what the problem is?" he asked as he sat down.

Rico picked up a lit cigar that had been resting in an ashtray on the desk, took a long drag, and exhaled. The cigar gave off a bouquet that brought to Guy's mind stale corn chips wrapped in old gym socks. Guy was used to the aroma of hand-wrapped Cubans, but Rico apparently preferred the gas station variety.

"Things are so much easier in Tijuana," Rico said. "Back home, if some *idiota* sticks his nose in your business, you just let him know you *mean* business. Problem solved." He took another puff of the blunt. "I do well for myself, everyone knows I'm not someone to be messed with. But *Tiyei* is small time. Pretty soon, I get too big. So I come out to Las Vegas. The big time. Supposed to be no rules out here. But there's a lot of fucking rules. I spend half what I made back home just in license fees. And then, after I follow all their bullshit, two nights ago they come in and try to shut me down. What is that shit? What the fuck is *moral turpitude*, anyway?"

"Oh," Guy said. "*That*. That is hard to explain."

"I don't need you to explain it," Rico said. "I just need you to tell me what to do."

"That depends. If they slapped you with a cease and desist, then you need to file an appeal. I mean right away. First thing tomorrow morning. In fact, you shouldn't even have this place open right now. The cops come back tonight, you go to jail. But if you file an appeal, you can keep this place open until the hearing. You'll probably lose, but it'll buy you the time you need."

"Time I need to do what?"

"Find a new base of operations. If you lose the appeal, they close this place for good. So you need a new location, new name, and..." Guy paused for a second. "A new owner."

"¿Qué?" It came out as a growl as Rico bit down his mustard-colored incisors on the head of his *el ropo*.

"Hear me out," Guy said. "The liquor and gaming board is never going to give a cabaret license to someone already accused of running a prostitution ring. Metro has a sheet on you now. You need to find a front man, a figurehead who's clean enough to get a license, who will act as the owner on paper. But since I'm guessing that you're not done living up to *su reputación* just yet, make sure it's someone expendable, someone whose mouth you can scare shut. So when the next club gets busted, he's the one who ends up doing eighteen months in NSP. When that happens, you just do the same thing all over again. Pack it up, move down the road. New owner, new license, no problem. Lather, rinse, repeat."

"What about my customers? If I move down the road, how do I make sure the johns follow?"

"Brand recognition," Guy said. "When the whales fly in with all that out-of-town cash, they don't want to waste it getting their dicks teased. They need someone to tell them where to find the sure thing. You invest a little in keeping the casino concierges and cab drivers on your side, and it won't matter where your club is or what it's called. They'll make sure the customers find it."

Rico nodded approvingly. "Now that kind of medicine I don't mind swallowing. You're a good guy to know. *¿De dondé eres?*"

"Nowhere."

"Nowhere?"

"You know." Guy shrugged. "Around."

"Well, stick around," Rico said. "And why don't you give me your number so if I need your services again, I can contact you directly. You know, without having to go through Shithead here."

"Jesus," Shady Mike mumbled under his breath.

"No, that's okay." Guy nervously ran his hand across the back of his neck. "Just call Mike. He'll get me the message."

"No, I'd rather deal with you direct. Come on, just give me your phone number so I can put it in the," he gestured to the Rolodex on his desk, "¿cómo se dice?"

"Trust me," Guy said. "It's better to go through Mike. I don't even own a telephone."

"Suit yourself," Rico said. "But consider yourself on retainer. As far as payment goes, I took care of things with Big Sal, so you don't need to worry about that anymore."

"Thanks." Guy's eyes wandered to the floor. "Also, I started a tab at the bar out there."

Rico laughed. "Yeah, I'll take care of that too. ¿Algo más?"

Guy shook his head. "Nope, that'll do it."

He stood up and turned to exit, but the sullen bouncer from the hall stepped into the room, blocking his path.

"Um, excuse me." Guy looked up at him, confused. "Did you also need some legal advice?"

Instead of answering Guy, the bouncer turned to Rico. "This twerp was harassing Brandi."

"Who's Brandi?"

On cue, the stripper from the bar appeared from behind the bouncer. Her mood had not improved.

"Oh," Guy said. "Hello again." He tried to sound gentlemanly.

Brandi ignored the greeting and called out to her boss. "This little faggot was keeping me from dancing with other customers. He owes me like fifty bucks for the time he wasted, and you oughtta throw him out of here for the shit he was saying to me."

"Not exactly how I recall the events in question," Guy said.

"Shut up, faggot!" Brandi spat at him.

The bouncer took a step closer to Guy.

"Hey!" Rico stood up for the first time since Guy had arrived. "He's a friend of mine."

"But Brandi said—"

8

"*¿Sabes lo que dije?*" The room shook as Rico bellowed the words. Everyone froze until Rico lowered his voice and calmly added: "I said he's a friend of mine."

The bouncer backed off, allowing enough room between him and the door for Guy to exit. Brandi just stood silently in disgust.

As Guy walked past, the bouncer leaned in toward him and growled under his breath. "You think you're some kind of tough guy?"

Guy shook his head calmly. "No, I'm not a tough guy. I'm the smart guy."

"Smart enough to run up five G's with Big Sal?"

"Smart enough to know when to keep my mouth shut." Guy turned back to Rico.

Rico shot the bouncer a look that left him thinking better of it. The bouncer's gaze fell to the floor and Guy took his cue to exit.

When they got to the parking lot, Shady Mike took a deep breath. "That mouth of yours is gonna get you killed one of these days."

"This mouth of mine is the only asset I have these days," Guy replied.

As Guy neared his faded Datsun 300ZX, Shady Mike reached into his pocket and pulled out a piece of notebook paper that had been hastily torn from its spiral binder.

"I forgot to tell you earlier," he started. "You got a call from some broad. Sounded pretty hysterical. Could barely understand her, she was so shaken up. Something about her sister missing. Said you'd know what she meant." He handed the paper to Guy. "It's a 213 number. That's LA, right?"

Guy stared at the piece of paper.

"Is that where you're from?"

Guy lifted his eyes from the paper.

Shady Mike corrected himself. "Sorry. That's right. You're from nowhere. My mistake."

Guy crumpled the piece of paper into his pocket and fumbled

for his car keys. "Do me a favor. Don't mention that phone call to anyone. Forget that area code too."

Guy opened the driver's side door to the Datsun and got behind the wheel. He put the key in the ignition, but before starting the engine, he rolled down his window and leaned out to Shady Mike.

"Make sure things get settled with Big Sal. I'm going to be out of touch for a couple days."

"Why?" Shady Mike's mouth hung open in a stunned expression. "Where are you going?"

Grateful for Shady Mike's steadfast obtuseness, Guy turned the ignition and put the transmission in drive.

"Nowhere," was his reply.

# CHAPTER 2

The Datsun pulled up to the curb in front of a Spanish-style single-story house in Eagle Rock a little after eight o'clock the following morning. Guy McCann had driven through the night, straight from the strip club parking lot, and crossed LA city limits before dawn. Arriving too early for a house call, he had checked into a motel in Culver City that let him pay the resident rate without asking too many questions. Being confined to the cramped single room, well stained with the remnants of past indiscretions, had driven him half goofy with anticipation. After an hour of restless pacing, Guy drove to a diner in Los Feliz to wait for the sun to come up. He spent sunrise staring at a plate of congealing eggs over easy while wondering how the waitress would react if he ordered something from the bar. But when he finally found himself standing on the porch steps, bathed in morning's first light, his eagerness dissipated, replaced by a paralyzing sense of hesitation. It required several deep breaths and false starts before he was able to lift his fumbling fingers from his pants pocket and ring the doorbell.

The door opened almost immediately, as if the occupant had also spent the last several hours in a state of unbearable urgency. Inside, a pale, doughy woman in her forties stood across the threshold. Guy forced a half-hearted smile.

"Hi Diane."

"Guy," Diane replied. An aversion to makeup and contemporary fashion made her look more world weary than she really was. Everything about her—hairstyle, wardrobe, mannerisms—seemed culled from a ladies' magazine someone might have picked from a supermarket checkout rack ten years ago. On top of that, if she had gotten a minute of sleep the night prior, it didn't show. Her appearance was so disorienting that Guy felt too uncomfortable to attempt any further small talk.

"I got your message," he told her. He kept his gaze just shy of her face.

Diane was staring at him with a stony expression, as if she were on tranquilizers. Only a fine tremor in her bottom lip betrayed her emotional state. She swung the door wide open for him to enter. Guy slowly crossed the threshold into the foyer.

He took in his surroundings. "Jesus," he reflexively muttered under his breath.

This was an observation, not an exclamation. When Diane Connor née Weston told others that the Lord was inside her home, she meant it literally. The image of Mary and Joseph's firstborn adorned every nook and cranny of the four-bedroom house. Against the walls: portraits in oils, watercolors, velvet. Cheap plastic novelty figurines lined every horizontal surface, such that every imaginable representation of the King of Kings was visible. Baby Jesus, Jesus on the cross, Jesus on the mount, Jesus healing the leper, Jesus handing out loaves and fishes. The longer Guy scanned the room, the more ridiculous the messianic scenarios became: Jesus teaching a school-age boy how to hit a curveball, Fly-fishing Jesus, Astronaut Jesus, Big-rig driving Jesus, Roller Derby Jesus, Disco Jesus, Harley Davidson Jesus, Hang Ten Jesus. If there existed some poseable action figure version with articulating limbs and matching playset—possibly Arctic Storm Jesus® (With Kung Fu Grip!)—Guy was confident it could be found in one of the kids' bedrooms, perhaps on furlough in Mary Magdalene's Malibu Dream House.

"I don't want to take up too much of your time," Guy said.

"I imagine you're pretty busy." He hoped his delivery didn't come off as sarcastic.

"Make yourself comfortable in the living room." Diane led Guy through the foyer. Guy doubted he could both be in the living room and be comfortable at the same time. "I'll get you a cup of tea," Diane said before departing to the adjoining kitchen.

Left to his own devices in the living room, Guy reluctantly took a seat on a faded corduroy-lined couch. As he sat down, he turned and was startled by the presence of a teenage girl, wearing a sullen expression and slumped over in the armchair next to the couch. She was staring at him with light blue eyes that were sunk far back in the sockets and surrounded by copious amounts of black eyeliner and mascara.

"Carol Ann," Diane called from the kitchen. "Say hello to Mr. McCann."

Instead of saying hello, Carol Ann continued to stare silently at Guy and he found himself locked in her empty gaze. Her skin was pale white, a stark contrast to the jet black dye in her hair. Carol Ann's lips were a deep crimson that, with her mouth hanging open ever so slightly, forced a resemblance to an inflatable sex doll. Without saying a word, or even changing the blank expression on her face, Carol Ann suddenly let her knees fall open and subtly cocked her head to one side, as if asking him a question.

Instinctively, Guy shook his head side to side. In response, Carol Ann shrugged, stood up, and walked out of the room. Guy's gaze followed her around the corner until it was interrupted by the sight of Diane returning from the kitchen with his cup of tea.

"Here you go." Diane extended the cup to him. Not knowing what else to do, Guy took a sip. It would be several minutes later before he fully processed what had just happened.

"I really appreciate your hospitality after...everything," Guy began. "But I think you ought to tell me what's happened. Time might be a factor here, so I hope you don't mind me being direct."

Diane opened her mouth to speak, but then stopped short. Her eyes were red and filled with tears. Guy checked the room for a box of Kleenex, saw none within eyeshot, and decided against taking the time to locate one.

"Diane," Guy said. "Where's Blair?"

She shook her head. "I don't know. Two nights ago she came here to the house. I hadn't seen her in over a year, since the trial." Her eyes fell to the teacup in her hand. "I had accepted that she didn't want a relationship with me. Not hearing from her all that time wasn't a surprise." Diane cleared her throat. "Her showing up on my doorstep out of the blue was the surprise. And Guy, if you had seen her…" Her wet eyes rose to meet his. "She didn't look well, and she sounded worse than I've ever heard her talk before. Rambling incoherently about this and that. All a mile a minute and none of it making any sense. She stayed the night with us. I had hoped she'd be here long enough that I'd be able to get her help, to make her better." Diane paused and her gaze fell to her lap. Tears were running down her pale, sagging cheeks. "But she was only here for the one night. The next morning, she was gone, and I haven't seen or heard from her since."

Guy furrowed his brow and tried to digest this information.

"Did she mention anyone?" Guy asked. "Anyone that she might have been staying with or spending time with?"

Diane shook her head. "She never mentioned any specific names of anyone. But she wasn't making any sense anyway. So, how would I be able to put together any of it if she had?"

"Did she leave anything behind?"

Diane pointed down the hall. "In the guest room, where she stayed the night."

"May I?" Guy rose from the sofa.

"Of course," Diane said. She began to sob.

Guy walked past her. He made his way down the hall to the guest bedroom at the far end of the house. He entered the room and looked around. It was a small room with a twin mattress ornately dressed in the corner. The walls were covered in faded pink patterned paper and more portraits of the carpenter from Nazareth, each hung in a location such that the likeness faced the bed in the corner. Guy didn't wonder much why Blair hadn't stayed in that room any longer than she did.

Aside from Diane's décor, nothing else occupied the room, except for an item resting on a nightstand next to the bed. Guy walked over and picket it up. A Polaroid OneStep. Guy examined the camera, peering into the viewfinder and inspecting the white plastic molding, tracing his index finger along the rainbow design that ran from the lens to the ejector slot. Finding nothing out of the ordinary about the camera, Guy placed it back on the nightstand and left the room.

Diane was waiting for him in the living room. She had stopped crying and was working on another cup of tea.

"Should I call the police?" she asked.

Guy shook his head. "Not yet." He thought for a second. "Give me a day or two first. She might be in the kind of trouble where we don't want them involved just yet."

"I'm sorry I didn't call you sooner," Diane said. "I know that the last time we talked, you said I should call you right away if I heard from Blair. But when she showed up, I was so overwhelmed that I didn't even think about it until after she left."

Guy reached his arm out to her, not so much as to comfort her but to cut her off. "You did the right thing," he said. "I just need to think this over for a little while."

"Do you want to stay here?" Diane asked. "You look like you've been driving all night. While you're in town you should stay with us. I insist."

Guy glanced at the space in the armchair that Carol Ann had occupied and shook his head.

"No, I don't think that would be a good idea," he said. "I'm staying nearby." He gave Diane the name and phone number of his motel. "Call me if you hear from Blair again."

15

Diane silently watched Guy leave the house. As he stepped through the doorway onto the porch, she called out to him. "What do you think she's gotten herself into this time?"

Guy paused. "It's Blair." He shook his head. "There's no way to know."

Within the hour, Guy was back in his motel, stripping out of the clothes he had been wearing for the last thirty-six hours and three hundred miles. After leaving Diane's house, Guy had made a few stops downtown, cautiously peeking into a few former haunts. But every time he walked back outside the bright southern California sunshine reminded him that he was wasting his time. He was unlikely to find any trace of Blair until after dark.

Back in his room, Guy opened a pack of plain white cotton T-shirts he had picked up at the 7-Eleven where he filled up his car on his way back to Culver City. He laid out one of the T-shirts on the edge of the bed and smoothed the palm of his hand over the crease that ran up the front of the shirt. He then lied down on the rough, threadbare bedspread that covered the creaky, uneven mattress, and tried to relax himself into a couple hours of sleep. After fifteen minutes of failure, he sat up, opened the drawer of the nightstand, and pulled out the bottle of Dewar's. Guy had impulsively bought the scotch at the same 7-Eleven, then relegated it to the nightstand drawer in self-disgust as soon as he had gotten back to his room. Now staring at the bottle, Guy thought to himself: *If she's in trouble, then I'm probably in trouble.* He put the bottle back into the drawer and tried not to touch it again.

The phone ringing woke him up. At first he couldn't tell where the noise was coming from, or why. He sat up and looked around, not altogether sure of his surroundings. It wasn't quite dark out, but it wasn't quite light out either, which added to his disorientation. His head was pounding. Was the ringing coming from outside his head or inside?

The phone rang again and he was finally able to locate the source. He reached to the floor and picked the receiver up off the cradle and held it to his ear.

"Look, I already told you," he mumbled. "It's not me making that noise. It's the asshole next door. He clearly has a serious drinking problem."

"Guy?" A female voice on the other end of the line. "What are you talking about?"

"Oh," Guy corrected himself. "Diane. How have you been?"

"Wha-what's go-going on?" Diane's voice was cracking. Suddenly, Guy heard Shady Mike's words in his head: *Could barely understand her, she was so shaken up.*

"Wait, what's happening?" His eyes were finally able to focus. He was becoming more aware that he was awake, that he was in a motel room in Los Angeles, why Diane was calling him. "Are you calling about Blair? Did you hear from Blair?"

"The hospital called." There was a breathless quality to her voice, and she was speaking in gasps. "She's in the emergency room on Beverly and San Vincente. The emergency room! She got there a few hours ago, they said. They said she was..." Diane stopped short of finishing the sentence, as if she physically couldn't get the word out.

Guy had already stopped listening anyway. He didn't feel drowsy or drunk anymore. He didn't feel anything but the beating of his heart in his chest. Guy hung up the phone, grabbed his clothes, and raced to the motel parking lot as fast as his legs would move him.

# CHAPTER 3

While the ER waiting room experience ranked among the most unpleasant of Guy's life, at least he found comfort in the accuracy of the cliché comparing it to some deep circle of hell normally reserved for serial child murderers and telemarketers. Shoulder to shoulder with the same societal dregs he had gone to law school to avoid, Guy kept an anxious eye on the door to triage. As he waited for someone to stick their nose out and tell him he could come on back, Guy took notice of the morbidly obese man next to him. This bloated whale was calmly thumbing through a heavily worn Harlequin romance novel, undeterred by the rip-roaring skin infection that had turned his calves into a pair of beet-red Doric columns. Guy glanced around and didn't see any volunteers pushing around a library cart, leading him to conclude that his plus-sized seatmate had at some point interrupted his trip to the ER to pick up some reading material to help pass the time once he arrived at the waiting room. This, in Guy's opinion, made this crimson-legged sea mammal the sanest and most forward-thinking person in the room.

"Guy McCann?"

He jerked his head away from the whale's cellulitic calves and rushed over to the triage window. Behind the glass, a disinterested nurse nodded toward the door leading back to the ER.

"Curtain Five," was all she offered.

The door buzzed and Guy instinctively pushed it open. Once inside, Guy realized that, in comparison, the waiting room had been a pacific oasis of serenity. He struggled to find his way through the packed emergency room, dodging impatient orderlies and delirious trauma victims, somewhat surprised that he was allowed to just wander around on his own through the chaos. He had expected someone to show him where to go, but no such Sacagawea presented herself. So after much trial and error, he realized that there were no patient rooms, per se, but rather curtained stalls housing gurneys, some vacant, most of them occupied. Each stall was numbered, but the number was inside the curtain, so it was impossible to tell which one was Curtain Five without peeking inside, often to the bemusement of the shabbily gowned occupant. After several *fuck offs*, from both patients and hospital staff alike, Guy found himself standing in front of what he was reasonably sure was Curtain Five.

But before he could summon the nerve to pull back the curtain and determine his accuracy, a young, prematurely balding man wearing surgical scrubs and an exasperated expression exited from inside the curtained stall, knocking into Guy.

"Jesus!" he exclaimed, taking Guy aback. The scrub-attired cue ball pushed past Guy, forcing Guy to rush alongside him to maintain his attention.

"Sorry." He struggled to keep pace through the crowded ER. "I'm here to see Blair Weston. Are you her doctor?"

"I'm *a* doctor," the man said. "And yes, I did just see Ms. Weston."

Guy paused, unsure of protocol. "I got a call from her sister. They said on the phone she was…"

"Raped?" The doctor's tone was surprising in both its candor and volume. He halted his hurried gait and turned to face Guy. "Yeah, that's what they told me too. Only I just finished examining her, and trust me, she wasn't assaulted."

"What?"

"That idiot ER resident ought to learn to open his ears for

once. I know it's busy down here, but that doesn't mean I need to do his job for him."

"What are you talking about?" Guy followed the doctor as he resumed his journey toward a nursing station by the exit. The doctor ignored Guy's question and instead bellowed at a white-coated man sporting a five o'clock shadow.

"Hey!" the first doctor yelled at the second. "Dr. Genius! Next time you feel like calling a GYN consult for a rape victim, make sure she was actually raped first."

The second doctor, simultaneously cradling two telephone receivers, one to each ear, while furiously pressing buttons on a pager that was alarming every five seconds, simply shook his head and extended a middle finger.

Guy turned to the first doctor with a confused look. "Excuse me," he began, reflexively adopting a litigious timbre to his voice. "I'm here because I got a call that Blair is in the hospital. You appear to be one of the doctors taking care of her. So, would you mind terribly just telling me exactly what the hell is going on here?"

The first doctor turned toward Guy. "The ER resident, aka Numbnuts McDouchebag over there—"

"Hey!" Guy heard the ER resident yell in response from the nursing station.

"Sorry, Numbnuts McDouchebag, *MD*," the GYN resident corrected. "He called me for a GYN consult, asking me to come down here with a rape kit because your girlfriend told them she was assaulted. But Dr. Dipshit doesn't know how to take a goddamn history. She didn't say she was raped. She said she was *penetrated*. She meant by a needle. Not by a..." He paused to rethink his word choice. "...a person."

"What?" Guy's eyes were darting back and forth at two doctors.

"Look," the GYN resident said, "I examined her, and there is no evidence of trauma whatsoever. So I asked her what the hell she was doing here. You know," his manner changed suddenly from matter-of-fact to something slightly immodest, "every once and a while we get this kind of thing in here. Some sick bird crying wolf just for the chance to be alone with a doctor. I'd like to say it doesn't, but between you and me, it happens."

"She's not exactly the type that needs to resort to that sort of thing to get male attention," Guy said.

"Says you." The GYN resident's voice quickly returned to its earlier deadpan delivery. "I only look at them from the waist down. But I'll take your word for it, because then she tells me that someone's been injecting her with drugs."

"Drugs?"

"With needles," the GYN resident said. "That's what she meant by penetration. She says someone's been sticking her with needles to inject her with drugs. In her sleep. That's why she thinks she needs medical attention."

Guy just stared at the GYN resident, trying to take in the information.

"While she was at it," the GYN resident continued, "she also mentioned that members of the mafia were following her, and that they were planting bugs in her apartment and in taxi cabs all over the city so they could spy on her." He cleared his throat. "She said they're the ones who have been drugging her." Then, in a whispered hush: "*They're trying to find out how much she knows.*"

Guy wrinkled his forehead. "That doesn't make any sense."

"*You think?*" The GYN resident threw his arms in the air. "Myself, I'd say that was pretty fucking insane. But what do I know? I'm just a doctor."

Guy stood there, unsure of how to respond. The GYN resident noticed his discomfort and softened his demeanor. "I'm sorry," he said, shaking his head. "I've been on for almost thirty hours. I'm a little...on edge."

Guy nodded stupidly.

"But let me ask you," the GYN resident continued, "does she have a history of mental illness?"

Guy tried to think of the best way to answer the question. "I know she likes to have a good time every once and a while."

The second doctor finally found himself liberated from the telephone and approached the GYN resident. "Don't even get started, I know what you're going to say," he began.

The GYN resident just shook his head. "You know my service is busy enough without this kind of bullshit."

"Usually when it's a psych patient, they get triaged to psych. When they get triaged for OB GYN, I call OB GYN. Fucking sue me."

The GYN resident rubbed his eyes with the heels of his hands. "I ought to kick your ass is what I ought to do. If I had the energy to do anything more than stand here listening to your bullshit, that is."

Guy frowned, becoming acutely aware that the situation showed no signs of resolving itself without his intervention. "Are you saying she needs a psychiatrist?" he asked. "She's lost her marbles or something?"

"Not exactly how we put it here in the ER," the ER resident said. "But, yes, we suspect she might be showing signs of mental illness. Which is why I called for a psych consult."

The GYN resident's eyes widened.

"Yeah," the ER resident added. "If you had stopped impugning my medical acumen for a minute, or if I could get a word in without my goddamn pager going off every two seconds, I would have told you that I called a psych consult twenty goddamn minutes ago. He's already down here seeing her. Look."

Both Guy and the GYN resident turned to see a third doctor approach. This one was dressed in a corduroy blazer and blue jeans, no necktie.

"Hey, which one of you is the ER resident?" the new doctor asked.

"Him." The GYN resident motioned to his right. Noting his wardrobe, he added: "You must be from psych. Here for the nutcase in Curtain Five?" Guy scowled in response, but all three doctors were blind to it.

"I just finished talking to her," the psych resident answered.

Guy decided to chime in. "You couldn't have been in there long."

"It didn't take long," the psych resident replied. "The urine tox isn't back yet, but she shows classic signs of a manic episode: paranoid delusions, self-referential thinking, mostly of a persecutory nature. She thinks some imaginary organized crime syndicate is out to get her. She's apparently been hiding out in a really ritzy hotel, trying to throw them off her trail, I guess. Who knows what else she's been blowing her money on. Reckless spending is typical in this scenario too."

"You seem pretty convinced that she's lost her mind," Guy said.

"It's all textbook stuff," the psych resident said. "Anyway, we're admitting her. She's not excited about the idea, so we're going to 2PC her."

"It means she's being committed to the pysch ward," the ER doctor explained to Guy.

"Committed?" Guy had trouble believing what he was hearing. "Do you really have justification for keeping her against her will?"

"It's a Catch-22," the psych resident said. "No one who needs an involuntary admission thinks they need an involuntary admission. The administrator on call has signed off on patients much less disturbed than her, trust me. We have to think about her safety. If we let her leave without a full evaluation and some period of observation, we don't know what kind of trouble she can get into."

"Can I see her?" Guy asked.

"Sorry," the psych resident replied. He manner offered a well-practiced dose of false sympathy. "We have security already escorting her upstairs. It would be better if you wait until visiting hours tomorrow. Intake upstairs is never pretty when it's an involuntary admission. Plus, security does not like it when you interfere with protocol."

"Yeah, but I'm telling you, her sister sent me over here to make sure she was all right," Guy explained. "She's been missing for the last two days and I want to see her to make sure she's okay."

"And I'm telling *you*," the psych resident shot back, "we're going to make sure she's okay. You can see her tomorrow when visiting hours start. On the twelfth floor. *Once visiting hours start.*"

Guy felt the back of his neck get hot, but he took stock of the three doctors flanking him and realized he wasn't going to win this argument. Not when he was outnumbered and they had home-field advantage. He peered over the psych resident's shoulder and saw that Curtain Five was pulled open. No sign of Blair, just an empty hospital gurney. Guy took a deep breath and accepted defeat.

The psych resident turned from Guy, satisfied that the conversation had ended. As he passed by the curtained area that Blair had occupied, the psych resident stopped and noticed a large brown paper bag on the floor.

"Shit," he said. "Escort forgot her belongings. I need to go catch them before they get upstairs."

The psych resident took off, and Guy realized the ER and GYN residents had also already split. He eyed the paper bag, glanced around, and saw that everyone in the ER was too busy to notice him. He walked over and squatted next to the bag, peeking inside. He found a faux-Louis Vuitton purse and opened it, quickly rifling through the contents. He pulled out a notepad and pen, both of which had the words *The Metropolitan Hotel* printed on them. He dug deeper and felt something hard and plastic. He pulled it out and saw that it was a hotel punch card key. He stood up quickly, palming the key before the psych resident returned with one of the security guards.

"There it is," the psych resident said, pointing to the bag as the guard scooped it up and disappeared back down the hallway.

Guy was confident that neither the resident nor the security guard had seen him going through the bag. Guy then jogged over and grabbed the psych resident before he had a chance to disappear again.

"Is there a phone I can use?" he asked.

The psych resident pointed to a pay phone on the wall near the exit. Guy hurried over to it, lifted the receiver to his ear, and dropped in a quarter. He held up the pen he had taken from Blair's purse, and dialed the number printed underneath the hotel logo.

A pleasant female voice answered. "Metropolitan Hotel, how may I direct your call?"

"Blair Weston's room?" His voice made it sound more like a question than a response.

"One moment."

There was a pause on the line. Guy held his breath, half expecting the receptionist to come back on the line to tell him there was no guest registered under that name. But instead, he heard a click and the line starting ringing. Not knowing what else to do, Guy held the line, listening to the extension ring as he held the receiver tightly to his ear.

Then a man's voice answered.

Guy froze.

"Hello?" the voice repeated.

Guy hesitated for a moment before speaking. "Blair, please."

"Who's this?" the voice insisted. Guy detected an urgency in the man's tone.

Guy panicked. "Um, this is Pacific Bell. Are you satisfied with your current long distance provider?"

"Is that the best you can do?" the voice replied. "You don't think the phone company would know it's calling a hotel room?" Then the line clicked.

*Admittedly not my best work*, Guy thought as he returned the receiver to the cradle. Ducking back into the hall of the emergency room, Guy spotted the psych resident heading down the corridor. Guy hurried to catch up to him.

"Excuse me," Guy said. "Do you know how long she'll be in the hospital?"

"It's a twenty-four-hour hold," the psych resident replied. "To give the inpatient team enough time to determine if she's dangerous to herself or others."

Guy smiled involuntarily, almost laughing out loud.

"What?"

"Nothing." Guy shook his head. "It's just…it won't take them twenty-four hours to figure that out."

# CHAPTER 4

"Excuse me." Guy was leaning in close to the receptionist at the front desk of the Metropolitan Hotel. "My wife has already checked into our room and I'm supposed to meet her up there. But I forgot the room number."

Guy's stomach was warm from the scotch he'd just finished at the lobby bar. It probably wasn't a coincidence that the dread that had lurked around him on the drive to the hotel had melted away. He hadn't liked the idea of leaving the hospital without seeing Blair, and he certainly didn't like the idea of who he might run into if he snuck into her hotel room. But Guy had to wait out the night before the psychiatry ward staff would let him see Blair and the only way he could do that and stay sane was by spending the time finding out what trouble she'd gotten herself into. And the only way he could will himself to do *that* was by first visiting the hotel lobby bar.

"Well, we're not permitted to disclose which rooms our guests are occupying," the receptionist recited through a rehearsed smile. "However, I can call the room so you can speak to your wife."

Her manicured fingertips hit a few buttons on the keyboard in front of her and the computer monitor came to life.

"Blair Weston," Guy said with a wink.

As the receptionist's fingers went to work on the keyboard,

Guy felt her eyes on him, making sure he wasn't trying to glance at the monitor. She then picked up a telephone resting on the counter in front of her and punched the room number onto the dial pad.

Guy stood and watched as the phone rang several times.

"I'm sorry." The receptionist allowed only the slightest trace of suspicion in her voice. "No one is picking up. Your wife doesn't appear to be in her room at the moment."

"She must have just stepped out," Guy said. "Well, if no one is in the room right now then I guess I'll just have to wait for her at the bar. Thank you for your assistance."

"Of course."

Guy winked at her again before turning and heading back toward the bar.

As soon as he gauged he was out of line of sight from the front desk, Guy darted for the elevator bank. He took the elevator to the seventh floor and without much difficulty found his way to the door marked 7466, the same four numbers that the receptionist had punched onto the telephone keypad when she rang Blair's room.

He knocked on the door and waited a beat. Just to be sure, he knocked again. Again, no answer. Guy pulled the punch key out of his pocket and slid it into the door's card slot. The lock clicked and Guy gently pushed the door open.

The room was silent. Guy crept in slowly, looking around. It was a junior suite, with a small sitting room and doors leading off to the bedroom and bathroom. Guy peered into the bedroom and noticed the bed was unmade. The dresser was cluttered with plastic orange pharmaceutical bottles and on the far corner was a stack of Polaroid photographs. Guy's mind flashed back to the instant camera he had found in Diane's guest room. As he approached the dresser, he noticed a perfume bottle. He picked it up and sniffed the nozzle. Once the fragrance caught his nose, Guy was certain he was in Blair's room.

Next, he picked up some of the pictures that sat on top of

the dresser and flipped through them. The pictures were of the inside of a Major League ballpark. The photographs had been taken from the stands behind the home dugout on the first base line. One of the ballplayers was in most of the pictures, a fresh-faced young man with broad shoulders and a large torso, wearing the home team's uniform. Guy flipped through the next several pictures and recognized they were of Blair standing in the ballpark bleachers. Guy noted two peculiarities that these last few pictures shared. First, in each of them, Blair's arm was extended, with her lower arm and hand out of frame, as if she had taken the photographs herself. The second peculiarity was less subtle: Blair's attire was in stark contrast to that of the surrounding fans in the stands. Instead of wearing baseball memorabilia, Blair was wearing an ornate antebellum Southern gown, complete with a black lace veil.

"Jesus," Guy muttered. He pocketed a few of the pictures, making sure to include one of Blair, and dropped the rest back on the dresser.

Just then, he felt a familiar sensation in his abdomen. The cumulative effect of the scotch and hospital coffee he had consumed over the last several hours knocked at his bladder. Guy gingerly entered the bathroom and, finding it empty, quietly walked past the shower stall, approached the toilet, and raised the seat. His anxiety level still high, Guy had difficulty relaxing enough to allow the passage of urine. However, after taking a couple deep breaths and conjuring some distracting images of faraway mountain streams, the tension dissipated and he began relieving himself. For a moment, Guy found himself at peace.

Then he heard the bathroom door swing closed behind him. Still midstream, Guy turned over his shoulder to the corner of the bathroom and saw a large, chisel-chinned gorilla of a man step out from the space previously hidden by the door.

"Let me guess," the gorilla grunted. "Ma Bell?"

Guy started fumbling with his zipper, trying unsuccessfully to squeeze off the flow of urine and silently cursing himself for not checking behind the door when he entered the bathroom.

"By all means," the gorilla said. "Take your time and finish."

"You sure?" Guy blurted.

"Do I look like I want your piss on me?"

Guy's heart rate continued to increase. "I drink a lot of coffee," he said. "So this might take a while. If you want to wait outside, I completely understand."

But as he said this, his stream slowed to a trickle. Guy futilely strained to prolong his urination for a few more seconds, but to no avail. In desperation, Guy turned around and faced the stranger occupying the bathroom with him, ignoring the fact that his flaccid penis was still sticking out his fly. "Wait a minute," Guy said. "I don't know what's going on here, but I'm sure we can work something out."

The gorilla looked down at Guy's crotch and shook his head in a mixture of pity and contempt. He took a step toward Guy and pulled a blackjack out of his coat pocket.

Guy's heart sank in his chest and he let out a sigh.

"Okay," Guy said. He stoically turned his back to his assailant. "Just not in the face, okay?" He leaned forward against the toilet tank, gripping the porcelain lid as he braced himself for impact.

The meaty fist holding the blackjack rose and readied to strike. As the gorilla took another step forward, Guy took a step back, pivoted, and swung the toilet tank lid as hard as he could. Guy had aimed for the head, but the lid weighed more than he had anticipated and ended up catching the gorilla in the shoulder instead. However, Guy hit him hard enough to knock him sideways, causing him to lose his footing. His weight and the force of Guy's blow created enough momentum to send him crashing through the glass door of the bathroom shower.

Guy stood frozen for several seconds before he was able to peer through the shattered shower door and peek at the figure sprawled in the tub. Embedded in his neck was a shard of glass measuring an inch wide. Blood was seeping from the edges of the wound and pooling around the bathtub drain. He was looking up at Guy, snarling.

"Well," he growled. "What are you waiting for?"

Guy glanced up and realized he was still gripping the toilet tank lid, holding the ten-pound piece of porcelain defensively above his head. If the gorilla hadn't said anything, Guy wasn't sure he would have thought of it himself.

Guy let the toilet tank lid swing down hard on the crown of the gorilla's head. The body fell limp inside the bathtub. Guy stared at the unconscious body, holding his breath and looking for signs of movement. Just to be sure, Guy poked at his head with the tank lid a few times, unable to produce a reaction.

Guy then dropped the lid at his feet and hurried out of the bathroom. His eyes darted around the hotel room, but he didn't see any sign that the gorilla had company. Guy grabbed the prescription bottles on the nightstand and pocketed them. He then walked to the hotel room door, opened it, and quickly exited, pausing only to hang the *Do Not Disturb* sign on the doorknob, as if by habit.

# CHAPTER 5

Dr. Happy was trying not to think about how uncomfortable he was but sitting out on the patio made it difficult. The late afternoon heat still hung over the Hollywood Hills, even though the sun was already starting to set, and he was starting to sweat through his wool suit. Everyone else at the party wore bathing suits, regardless of whether they were spending time in the pool or just reclining in one of the lounge chairs or hanging out by the tiki bar. The young men wore board-style shorts, although very few of them actually surfed. The women wore string bikinis, the tops unashamedly displaying perfectly formed breasts. Dr. Happy's indifferent gaze followed the male and female partygoers alike as they passed, mentally dividing them into two camps: those who were naturally gifted and those who had medical assistance.

It was a hardwired reflex, one he couldn't suppress if he tried, but at least it took his mind off the heat. He subconsciously deduced among the women not only which breasts were augmented and which were not, but what cup size they were and, based on the size of the gap in the cleavage, what size they used to be. When the young men swaggered by, he inspected their arms for track marks if they were suspiciously thin. If they were suspiciously well built, for varicose veins and body acne. Along the surface of the ample supply of visible flesh, he looked for asymmetric moles with irregular borders. He checked for calluses on the backs of the girls' index fingers, a telltale sign of bulimia. Teardrop-shaped asses told him which girls were on the pill. Of course, this only worked with the actresses. The models were too anorexic to menstruate. And if they did take birth control, they also took diuretics to keep the water weight off.

He was not being paid for poolside diagnoses, of course, but these observations did pass the time.

He took note of a thin blonde, a sarong knotted at her hip, walking over to him from one of the open-air cabanas scattered around the pool. She had a perfectly symmetrical face and flawless, evenly tanned skin. Like all the other guests at the party, she had a twenty-two-gauge intravenous catheter in the cephalic vein of her left forearm.

"Dr. Happy." Her voice came out as a warm murmur. She tucked her hair around her ear with her right hand as she leaned over to him. "I need some more."

Dr. Happy motioned to the chair next to him and she sat down. He turned to her and grabbed her wrist with his index and middle fingers. As he felt her pulse, he watched her sternum rise and fall, silently counting to himself. After thirty seconds of this, he reached into a black leather bag at his feet and produced a penlight.

"Keep your eyes open," he instructed.

In a pendulous motion, he swung the light from one of her eyes to the other, watching her pupils constrict and dilate in turn.

"Count backwards from one hundred by sevens," he asked her absently.

She recoiled from him slightly. "Why?"

"Just do it," he answered firmly.

"Okay." She sighed. "One hundred, ninety-three, eighty— wait, why am I doing this?"

He lowered the penlight and faced her. "Repeat after me," he said. "*No ifs, ands, or buts.*"

"What?" Her nose scrunched up as if she smelled something

unpleasant. "This is dumb. Why are you asking me this stuff?"

He gave up and dropped the penlight back into the bag. "Okay. You can have some more," he relented. "But not *a lot* more."

Dr. Happy pulled a vial from his bag and drew up a small amount of clear fluid into a plastic syringe. He then motioned for the girl to get closer. Once she complied, he twisted the tip of the syringe into the Hep-Lock at the end of her IV and slowly pushed two milligrams of lorazepam into the blonde's circulatory system.

The blonde giggled. She closed her eyes and leaned further forward, close enough to kiss him.

"Thanks," she whispered.

She stood up and wobbled back toward the pool.

Dr. Happy dropped the syringe into the red container next to his chair and turned his attention back to the other partygoers when the pager clipped to his belt started beeping. He read the number on the display and winced. He tasted a warm bitterness in the back of his throat as he stood up and made his way into the house. The kitchen was just adjacent to the rear entrance, and inside it he found a phone secured to the near wall. He lifted the receiver and with his index finger quickly worked the rotary dial. The other line picked up after only one ring.

"Hey," Dr. Happy said. "You paged?"

The voice on the other end was curt. "We got a wounded soldier. Needs a friendly doc."

"Uh huh." He absently peered out the window at the girls in the pool outside.

"How soon can you get downtown?"

He checked his wristwatch. "I'm in Hollywood. An hour, maybe?"

"Make it a half hour, okay? The Metropolitan. Room 7466."

"What can I expect?"

"Bobby's cut pretty bad. Bring a needle and thread. A lot of thread." The voice paused. "And something to take the edge off. That's your specialty, right?"

He didn't reply.

"So beat your feet, all right? To hear him explain it, you'd think Bobby'd been cut in half."

He pushed aside one of the venetian blinds shading the kitchen window to get a better look at the blonde as she unwrapped the sarong from her waist and gingerly stepped into the shallow end of the pool. "Who cut him?" he asked.

"How is that any of your fucking concern?" the voice barked. The line clicked.

Dr. Happy broke his gaze from the blonde and glanced down at the receiver in his hand. He took a deep breath and hung up the phone. Back outside, he approached the host of the pool party, a tall, lanky kid with shaggy brown hair who couldn't have been a day over nineteen.

"I've got to go," Dr. Happy said.

"What?" the kid asked blankly. "Oh, okay man. Well, thanks again." He flashed a goofy grin.

He sighed. "I've got to go," he repeated.

The light bulb finally went on. "Oh! Okay, man. Hold on." The kid dashed to the other side of the patio, grabbed one of the male guests, and whispered something into his ear. He then quickly jogged back, extending one of his arms. In his hand was a roll of one-hundred-dollar bills held together with a rubber band.

"Here you go," the kid said, tossing him the roll. "We're cool, right?"

Dr. Happy quickly flipped through the bills. "Miles Davis," he replied. "And do yourself a favor and keep them away from the deep end." He motioned toward the blonde and her friends in the pool. "You don't want a Natalie Wood situation on your hands."

The kid shot him a confused look and then smiled. "Hey, man. We're having another party next weekend in Malibu. Hawaiian Tropic chicks are gonna be there. You should come by."

He squinted back at the kid. "I'll check my calendar."

"Okay." The kid shrugged. "So, can I tell people you're

coming?"

"I'll check my calendar." He said it slower this time.

"Okay, man," the kid replied. "Cool. Hey, thanks again for coming, man. Really appreciate it. You want a drink for the road?"

He shook his head. "No thanks." He turned back toward the house. In all his years practicing medicine, both on the level and off, Dr. Happy never got used to being treated so nicely by people he couldn't stand to be around.

As he drove down the hill toward city center, Dr. Happy recalled noticing the visibly enlarged nodes along one side of the shaggy-haired party host's neck. He knew it most likely represented a resolving case of mononucleosis, but with any luck it could be lymphoma instead.


The first thing Dr. Happy noticed when he arrived at room 7466 was the *Do Not Disturb* sign hanging on the doorknob. He checked up and down the hallway, wondering if he was being set up. But then he noticed that the door had been left slightly ajar, just enough so he could push it open without a key. He let the door swing fully open before he stepped into the hotel room. In his right hand was his black leather medical bag. With his left he pulled a small handcart, upon which was strapped a large catalog case. Once inside the hotel room, Dr. Happy noticed the drops of blood on the carpet, leading away from the door and across the sitting room carpet. He closed the door, left the handcart in the foyer, and followed the blood trail to the bathroom, where he found Bobby lying in the bathtub, the shard of glass still stuck in his neck.

"You a doctor?" Bobby asked.

"Well, I'm not housekeeping." Dr. Happy set his bag down on the vanity countertop. "Otherwise both our days would be taking a turn to shit."

Dr. Happy crouched down and examined the wound on

Bobby's neck, and the piece of glass six inches long and one inch wide jutting out of it.

"Any trouble breathing?"

Bobby slowly shook his head. Dr. Happy reached for Bobby's wrist and felt his pulse.

"You fell through the glass into the shower?" Dr. Happy asked.

Bobby nodded.

"Then you walked out to the sitting room, called Rip, and then left the room door open for me?"

Bobby nodded again.

"And then you walked back to the bathroom and got back in the tub?"

"Yeah," Bobby grunted. "What about it?"

"Why did you get back in the bathtub?" Dr. Happy asked.

"I don't know," Bobby answered. "I guess I didn't want to get my blood all over the hotel room."

Dr. Happy brought a hand to his brow and squeezed his eyes shut. "You could have done me a favor and got onto the bed while you had the strength. Now I have to carry you over there."

"Yeah," Bobby replied in an irritated tone. "I'm terribly sorry about the inconvenience."

Dr. Happy took note of the time on his watch and returned his attention to Bobby.

"Do you take any blood thinners?"

"What?"

"Aspirin, Coumadin, dipyridamole, take any of that?"

"Nah."

"Do you have any medical conditions I should know about?"

"Yeah, I got a medical condition."

"Which would that be?" Dr. Happy asked.

"I can't remember the technical term for it," Bobby said. "But it's that thing where a piece of fucking glass gets stuck in your goddamn neck. You ever hear of that one, doc?"

"Okay." Dr. Happy figured that was about as forthcoming

as Bobby was going to get.

He rose to his feet and picked up the folded bath towels that sat on the brushed nickel rack above the toilet, then walked with them out of the bathroom, grabbing his bag on the way. He went to the bedroom, placed his bag on the nightstand, and stripped the bedspread and sheets off the mattress. He then laid out the towels on top of the bare mattress, smoothing them out to make sure the entire surface was covered. Once he was satisfied with his workspace, he walked back to the bathroom.

"Can you stand?" he asked.

Without waiting for an answer, Dr. Happy squatted down just outside the bathtub, grabbed Bobby's hand, and pulled the arm opposite the stab wound around his own neck. He stood up slowly, lifting Bobby into a standing position. He then half carried him from the bathroom to the bed, making sure not to touch the piece of glass. As soon as he had Bobby lying down on top of the bed, Dr. Happy reached into his leather bag, retrieved a pair of trauma scissors, and cut off Bobby's shirt. Once this was done, Dr. Happy walked over to the foyer and retrieved the hand cart. After unzipping the catalog case, he pulled out a pair of two individually packaged plastic syringes, two hypodermic needles, an ampule of lidocaine, an IV start kit, and a liter bag of saline, laying them all out on the side of the bed next to Bobby.

"The first thing I'm going to do is place an IV."

Bobby winced. "I'm afraid of needles."

"Or I could leave, and you could hang out here until the guests next door call the front desk to report the funny smell."

"All right, all right." The gruffness of his voice started to retreat. "Do what you need to do, doc."

Dr. Happy quickly placed an eighteen-gauge angiocath in Bobby's antecubital vein and attached a stretch of plastic tubing that connected to the bag of saline. He hung the saline bag from one of the bedposts and stood watching the fluid drip from the bag for a few seconds. Dr. Happy pulled his stethoscope and blood pressure cuff from his leather bag, then manually checked

Bobby's blood pressure and pulse. He pulled a small notebook out and wrote down the time and Bobby's vital signs. He then peered into the catalog case and produced a vial marked remifentanil hydrochloride.

"Your opinion of me is going to significantly improve in about thirty seconds," Dr. Happy said. He opened one of the syringes and injected the anesthesia, watching as the contempt washed away from Bobby's face.

"Fuckin' A, doc," he cooed. "You are the tits, man."

"They all say that." Dr. Happy picked up one of the glass ampules of two percent lidocaine solution and cracked open the neck. "But when they see my bill, they call me something else entirely."

He opened another syringe from its sterile packaging and twisted the tip into the hub of a large bore needle. After uncapping the needle, he stuck it through the neck of the bottle of lidocaine, pulling back on the syringe's plunger to draw up the bottle's contents. He gave the syringe a tap with his forefinger and pushed in the plunger, expelling the air and a small amount of lidocaine in an arcing stream. Dr. Happy then leaned over and stuck the needle into Bobby's skin, injecting small amounts of lidocaine around the perimeter of the wound until the syringe was empty.

"That's the best I'm going to be able to do," he said. "It looks like you managed to avoid any damage to your trachea, and I doubt you hit either your carotid or your jugular, because you wouldn't still be alive in you had. But once I take the glass out, I'm still going to have to go in there and explore for any internal damage that needs to be surgically repaired. But I'm not set up to put you under entirely, so you're going to have to be awake for this. My advice is that you keep your eyes closed."

"Right on, doc," Bobby murmured.

Dr. Happy then ripped the top of the sterile packaging of a blue surgical towel and laid the towel out on the bed in front of him, careful not to let anything touch the top surface. He then rapidly tore open a suture kit, a set of surgical gloves, a stainless steel probe, a bottle of saline solution, and a roll of gauze, never touching the contents but instead allowing them to drop onto the surgical towel. He then turned his attention back to the shard of glass. Lacking a second set of hands, he thoughtfully planned out his next several moves. After a few seconds of deliberation, he donned the left surgical glove and with that hand took a fistful of gauze.

With the index finger and thumb of his right hand, he carefully squeezed the tip of the shard of glass. In one slow, smooth motion, he pulled the shard free, immediately covering the wound with the gauze with his left hand. He inspected the jagged glass for a moment and then, convinced that he had managed to extract it all in one piece, carefully placed it on the nightstand.

After a few attempts, he wriggled his right hand into the leftover surgical glove. He then picked up the stainless steel probe, lifted the gauze, and started exploring.


Some hours later there was a knock at the door. Dr. Happy removed his surgical gloves and approached the peephole. When he saw who was on the other side, his face contorted and the acid in his gut started to rise again. After a deep breath, he opened the door. In the hallway stood a tall, well-tanned man with a lithe, wiry frame. He wore a pale blue Armani suit that fit him like a second skin over a silk shirt whose open collar revealed an ample amount of well-groomed chest hair. His dark hair was greased back in a classic Italian Mafioso look; however, Dr. Happy had difficulty accepting that Rip Mancuso—despite his couture, coif, and surname—was actually Italian. Dr. Happy considered Rip more closely related to the stout, an invasive species of weasel known for its territorial behavior and surplus killing. And those came from Northern Europe.

Rip entered the suite, walking past Dr. Happy as if he wasn't there.

"He's lost some blood," Dr. Happy reported. "So I started some IV fluids. Luckily the glass missed any major vessels. I threw in some—"

"Is he going to live?" Rip cut him off, his back turned to Dr. Happy.

"Yes." Dr. Happy reflexively lowered the volume of his voice.

Rip walked over to where Bobby was lying on the bed and observed Dr. Happy's handiwork. His neck was sewn up and surgical dressing had been applied. The remifentanil was wearing off and Bobby was drifting in and out of consciousness. Rip slapped him across the face.

Bobby jerked his eyes open.

"Who was it?" Rip asked matter-of-factly.

Bobby blinked several times until Rip's visage came into focus. "The guy who did this?" Bobby motioned to his neck. "Never saw him before." He coughed as he spoke. "Tall guy. Dark hair."

"Anything else?"

"Big mouth," Bobby added.

"Out of towner?"

"Maybe."

"Well, he's a dead man, anyway," Rip said. "What did he want with the girl?"

"Don't know."

"He take anything?"

"How would I know? Been bleeding in a bathtub since he left."

Rip performed a walkthrough of the bedroom before heading to the sitting room. Noticing a fine residue of white powder on top of the coffee table, Rip ran a finger across its glass surface and rubbed it against his gums.

"Yeah, we gotta find this little cunt quick." Rip ran his tongue over his teeth and spat onto the carpet. "For real." He let his gaze drift from the hotel interior to the city view displayed outside the portrait window of the sitting room. The sun was about to come up, the twilight casting a glow on the buildings and streets below.

"Bobby's done bleeding," Dr. Happy said, "but he could stand to get some packed cells."

Rip's face wrinkled in response, but he kept his eyes fixed on the sprawling Los Angeles landscape outside the window.

"Blood transfusion," Dr. Happy clarified. "I can get a couple pints in a few hours, then come back here and hook him up. Or are you taking him somewhere else?"

"I checked with the front desk," Rip answered over his shoulder. "The cunt has this room booked through the rest of the week. Might as well keep him holed up here for now."

Dr. Happy went to the bathroom and washed his hands. When he returned to the bedroom, Rip was looking through the Polaroid pictures on the bedroom dresser.

"Does he really need the blood?" Rip asked without looking up from the pictures.

"He's showing signs of early hypovolemic shock. Tachycardia, thready pulse, skin and nail bed pallor, plus he keeps—"

"Jesus!" Rip threw the photographs back onto the dresser and faced Dr. Happy for the first time since he entered the hotel room. "Are we paying you by the hour? Just answer the goddamn question."

Dr. Happy felt his jaw click. "Yes," he replied. "He needs the blood."

"Then go get it," Rip said. "I'll stay and keep an eye on him."

"While I'm gone, he might..." Dr. Happy began.

"I said go get it," Rip snapped. The indifference to Dr. Happy's presence was gone from his eyes, replaced with a fixed, steely glare that seemed to silently order Dr. Happy out of the hotel room. Dr. Happy complied without further comment.

On his way out, Rip called out to him. "One more thing, doc." Rip took one of the pictures of Blair from the dresser and showed it to him. "If you happen to spot this little cunt during your travels, make sure you let me know."

Dr. Happy glanced at the picture, noting her atypical attire.

In his mind, she resembled a strung-out version of Scarlett O'Hara.

*All this commotion over her?* Dr. Happy asked himself. *She looks like a goddamn lunatic.*

# CHAPTER 6—September 13, 1985

"You're a legal eagle now," Milloy said. He slid Guy's bourbon and Coke aside and replaced it with a neatly poured scotch. "No more eating kids' meals."

Guy McCann grimaced. "I can't drink that straight." Guy rose from his chair. "At least have the bartender put some ice in it."

"*Nyet*," Milloy placed a hand on Guy's shoulder and pushed him back into his seat. He slid over in his chair so he was facing Guy. "The training wheels are off my friend." Milloy raised his own glass. "Here be dragons."

The glasses clinked together and Guy took a reluctant swig. As soon as the alcohol hit the back of his throat, he felt his esophagus spasm.

"Ack!" He covered his mouth with a corner of the tablecloth to prevent from spraying its contents across the room.

Milloy laughed. "You really put the *junior* in junior partner, partner."

Guy shook it off. He sat back in his chair and glanced around the nightclub, trying to take it all in. It was the first time he had been in a private club, and before stepping inside that evening, he hadn't thought they still ran places like this. Doormen in tails, waiters wearing white gloves. And glancing around at the clientele, Guy had the impression the club was restricted. The tables were occupied by well-fed men with heavy jowls and graying temples. Guy was by far the youngest male patron. The women, on the other hand, were all young, lithe, dressed to kill. Most of them were littered throughout the room, typically occupying the company of three or four of the older men at a time. Along the bar, the rest of them were lined up, as if on display.

Only one of the women in the club appeared a day over twenty-one, and she was probably pushing forty, by Guy's estimation. Not that he would argue with giving her a throw though. She carried a matronly air about her, snapping comments at the younger girls in a European-sounding accent that Guy couldn't quite place. Her blonde hair was tightly pulled back into a meticulous bun, a dated look that somehow managed to seem stylish in a classic retro way compared to the blown-out modern look that the other girls were sporting. She carried her buxom frame with confidence, displaying just enough cleavage to imply a concealed sexuality that, once coaxed out of hiding, offered the unmistakable advantages of experience.

The blonde held Guy's attention as he watched her walk along the bar. That is, until she passed by the dark-haired girl at the end of the row, at which point his gaze stopped dead in its tracks. Guy's pupils dilated involuntarily as he took her in. This raven-haired enchantress. In an instant, he had forgotten all about the matronly blonde. In fact, he completely lost awareness of the presence of anyone else in the room.

The girl must have noticed him staring because her eyes glanced over and caught his. Embarrassed, Guy jerked his head away, failing to appear nonchalant and instead just drawing more attention to himself as he almost knocked his glass over in the process. This made her smile.

"Wow, that was smooth." Milloy frowned at Guy's lack of delicacy. "I see your game involves breaking the ice by making them think you have some sort of palsy. What do you do to seal the deal, piss your pants?"

"Shut up." Humiliated, Guy turned his attention back to his

drink. After choking down a few gulps, he focused back on Milloy. "Do you know that girl?" Guy motioned toward the new-found object of his obsession. "Have you seen her here before?"

Milloy shook his head. "Must be new in town." He dipped his pinky into his scotch and brought it to his tongue. "But that's a good thing. New model, original parts." He looked back at Guy. "You're in the market. Why don't you go over there and kick the tires? Maybe she'll let you take her for a test drive."

Guy's heart started racing in his chest.

"Or is that like giving the keys to a Lamborghini to a kid who just got his learner's permit?" Milloy laughed cruelly.

Guy scowled. "I've logged plenty of hours behind the wheel, trust me."

"Yeah," Milloy chided. "Prove it." He jerked his head in the direction of the girl at the end of the bar. "First paycheck says you stall just trying to get in first gear."

"Uh-uh." Guy smiled awkwardly, straining to come up with another automobile reference suitable for the situation. After a few seconds of thinking he announced: "I can handle this one on cruise control."

He approached the bar and shyly made eye contact with the dark-haired girl. He dropped his arms to his sides and discreetly wiped the sweat from his hands onto his pants.

"Hi," Guy began, carefully delivering the word to make sure his voice didn't crack. "I was wondering if you've been hit on by enough men this evening. Because if not, I'd like to offer my services." He extended his arm. "I'm Guy McCann."

She smiled in a way that seemed like it was in spite of herself. Guy couldn't tell if she was acting the part or not. But when she extended her arm to meet his, he stopped caring.

"I'm Blair." She spoke softly but confidently. "And your offer is very enticing. But how do I know that after a couple of miles you won't just trade me in for a higher end model?"

Guy's face flushed and he silently cursed Milloy's big mouth. He considered aborting before deciding that it was impossible to feel more humiliated than he already did.

"Something tells me I'm already looking at the luxury model," Guy recovered. A cocky grin found its way to his lips as a sudden sense of bravado came over him.

"You sure that's something you can afford?"

"Oh," Guy hesitated. "Are you going to ask for a down payment?" *Is that how this works?*

Blair tilted her head. "I didn't mean financially."

Guy still didn't know what she meant, but he decided to switch the topic. "Um, would you care to join me at my table?" he asked.

"You and your friend?" Blair lifted a finger toward Milloy, who was still occupying his seat and his scotch at the table.

"No, just me," Guy said. "He's leaving."

"Does he know that?"

"He'll figure it out."

Guy escorted Blair to the table and they both sat down. Smiling coyly, Milloy extended an arm to Blair, which Guy intercepted and pinned to the table.

"*Get the fuck out of here,*" Guy told Milloy.

Milloy mouthed *okay* in a theatrical act of capitulation. He picked up his drink and left, making his way toward the far end of the bar.

Guy turned to Blair and smiled. "Told you he'd figure it out," he said. "He's a smart guy."

"I admire that level of intuition," Blair replied. "He must kill with the ladies."

"If by 'kill' you mean 'is tolerated by,' and by 'the ladies' you mean 'whatever he can find cruising Hollywood Boulevard after dark,'" Guy answered, "then yes, you have him pegged."

A moment of silence, and Guy suddenly realized what was missing from the picture.

"What are you drinking?" He flagged the waiter over to the table.

"Whatever you're enjoying," she said. In response, the waiter turned his attention to Guy.

Guy furrowed his brow. "This is straight scotch." He looked at his glass indignantly. "I doubt you'd—"

"What he's having," Blair instructed the waiter.

Guy laughed as the waiter departed for the bar. "You'll be sorry."

"I wouldn't invest too much time worrying about it." She leaned in toward him, resting her arms on the table. "So, Guy McCann," she began, "how do you keep yourself busy?"

"You know those scumbag lawyers you see in late-night TV commercials, chasing ambulances and hitting up car companies over exploding gas tanks?"

"Yeah," Blair said. "You're one of those?"

"Not yet." Guy crossed his fingers. "But someday."

Blair grimaced. "You're really a lawyer, though?"

"Just passed the bar. We're here celebrating." He gingerly sipped from his glass. "That and networking. Maybe find a couple of clients for our burgeoning practice."

"I don't think you'll find too many exploding gas tanks in here," Blair said.

"Probably not."

"But if I were you, I wouldn't bother representing the guy with the car that blew up," Blair said. "I'd be looking to land the guy who owns the car company."

"I like the way you think."

Blair playfully bit her bottom lip. "You might want to spend a little more time in deliberation before you deliver that verdict."

The waiter returned with Blair's scotch.

Guy eyed Blair's glass. "You know, you don't have to try to impress me."

Blair lifted the glass and downed its contents, somehow making the act appear graceful. "You mean, I don't have to try *very hard*." There was not a note of harshness to her voice.

Guy glumly faced his own drink and forced down its remains. He had to put all his effort in clamping shut the muscles in the back of his throat to keep down the scotch.

Blair observed this and her eyes narrowed, as if she were about to say something disparaging, but then her look softened and she instead changed the subject. "I just read something that said there are more students in law school today than there are practicing lawyers."

"Yeah, I've heard that."

"Well, call me crazy," Blair said, "but doesn't that mean we're headed for critical mass?"

"You're crazy," Guy countered with a smile. "There can never be such a thing as too many lawyers. We live in a litigious society, and it's just going to get better."

"*Better?*"

"In twenty years, women are going to need to sign a release before a guy is allowed to hit on them in a bar. Otherwise he's going to get slapped with a six-figure sexual harassment suit and a restraining order. You won't be able to go anywhere without your own general counsel and a public notary. It's going to be beautiful."

"That's really your idea of beautiful? And I'm crazy?"

"Yeah, you're crazy," Guy replied. "And no, that's not really my idea of beautiful."

"Then what is?"

Guy leaned forward, but before he could answer, the buxom older blonde that Guy earlier had spotted by the bar approached the table. Standing over Blair with an expression reminiscent of a puritanical schoolmarm, the woman's mere presence caused Blair's demeanor to change instantaneously. Guy felt the temperature of the room drop by several degrees.

"Excuse me," Blair said softly, her eyes directed downward. She rose from her chair and followed the blonde to a corner of the room.

Guy slowly stood up and walked back to the bar, keeping his eyes fixed on the two women. The blonde was speaking to Blair in a sharp tone, although Guy couldn't hear what she was saying over the din of the crowded room.

He approached Milloy at the bar and nudged his arm.

"Who's that?" Guy gestured toward the blonde.

"That's Anneleise Casparo."

"Why does that name sound familiar?"

"You've probably heard of her husband."

Guy shook his head. "What does he do?"

"Don't you read the papers? He's what we call a *respectable businessman*." As he said this, Milloy slowly pushed his nose to one side with his index finger. "He's the big fish I've been trolling for ever since I first hung up my shingle."

Guy paused. "You mean he's connected?"

"Uh-uh," Milloy replied. "He *is* the connection."

Guy's forehead wrinkled. "Doesn't representing that kind of clientele bother you?"

"What are you asking me? Does money bother me?" He shook his head. "No, it does not."

Guy watched as Anneleise Casparo finished speaking her mind. Blair had not uttered a single word in response. Turning from her, Anneleise headed back across the far side of the room. Guy tried to judge from her expression if she was satisfied with the outcome of their one-sided conversation, but failed.

Blair approached Guy with a smile that seemed like it was cut out of a toothpaste ad.

"It was a genuine pleasure meeting you." The charm had been drained from her voice, replaced with a pleasant but formal, almost robotic, quality. "But I'm afraid I'm needed elsewhere."

"Needed for what?" Guy asked.

But instead of answering him, she walked away.

# CHAPTER 7—September 30, 1987

Guy had switched from scotch to coffee and had been driving around LA all night. Too anxious to sleep and too paranoid to stop moving, he cruised aimlessly from the 110 to the 405 to the 605 to the 101. Occasionally he would take an off-ramp and find a 7-Eleven to piss and refuel. He didn't know what else to do but stay on the move until morning and go back to the hospital as soon as visiting hours started.

As the sun started peeking up over the hills, he grew more anxious. He had made it through the night, but was Blair safe? Whoever that gorilla was back in Blair's hotel room, did he know she was in the hospital? Was he in any shape to tell anyone?

As he pulled his car into the hospital parking lot, these thoughts were pushed to the back of his mind and replaced by his desire to see Blair. He hurried through the main lobby on the ground level of the hospital, following signs to the elevators. Guy entered one of the elevators and pushed the button for the twelfth floor. However, the button failed to light up and the elevator stood still. He pressed the button several times to no effect. Banging and kicking the control panel was similarly futile. Guy stepped back into the lobby, out of breath. Guy stopped at the information desk and loudly drummed his fists on the countertop to get the attention of the bored-looking girl on the other side.

"Hey," Guy said. "Are those elevators not working?"

"Those elevators?" The girl was chomping on a piece of bright pink bubblegum so hard it made her oversized hoop earrings sway back and forth like two plastic porch swings hanging from her earlobes. "They work."

Guy frowned. "Well, I was trying to get to the twelfth floor to visit a friend and they weren't working."

"You going to the psych unit?" The girl raised an eyebrow. "It's a locked unit. You can't go up without an escort. You have to call for someone to come down and let you in. They have a special key that makes the elevator go to the twelfth floor. You can't get up there without it."

"That's fascinating," Guy said, less than thankful for his newfound working knowledge of hospital elevators. "Could you call up there so they can send someone down for me?"

The girl pointed to a courtesy phone attached to the wall next to him. "It's extension 6-1212."

Guy sighed. "You've been incredibly helpful."

"You think so?" Her eyes brightened. "Because if you could write that on one of these comment cards that would totally get me out of dutch with my supervisor." The girl reached behind the desk and earnestly handed Guy a pamphlet printed on light blue card stock, folded into thirds. On the cover were printed the words "Your Comments Count!"

Guy held up the comment card. "Oh, yeah." He flashed a sardonic smile. "I would absolutely love to write—" He abruptly ended midsentence and tore the card in half, letting the pieces drop to the floor. He turned his back to the girl and picked the courtesy phone receiver off its cradle, indifferent to her stunned expression.

A bored female voice picked up. "Reception."

"Extension 6-1212, please."

The line clicked and the call went through. After a few rings, another female voice came through the receiver with the same rote delivery. "Psychiatry."

"Hello." Guy tried to sound relaxed. "My name is Guy McCann. I'm downstairs in the lobby to see Blair Weston. She was admitted yesterday."

"What was that patient's name again?"

"Blair Weston," Guy repeated.

"Please hold." Guy noticed a rushed quality to her voice.

Guy tapped his foot rapidly as he waited. He turned back toward the girl working the information desk, who detected his gaze and immediately rewarded his attention by giving him the finger. Half noticing, Guy turned back to face the phone.

"Um," the receptionist began after returning to the line, "I think…" her voice became muffled, as if she had covered the receiver with her palm. Guy heard murmuring in the background, coming from two distinct voices. One of them, a male voice, said something with a worried tone.

The receptionist quickly returned to the line. "The doctor will be right down." She still sounded anxious.

"Is everything okay?" Guy asked.

The line clicked and Guy hung up, his nerves on edge more than ever.


Dr. Happy had arrived at the hospital an hour after sunrise, knowing that Frank Castle came off duty from the psychiatric inpatient unit at change of shift and was therefore unavailable before seven o'clock. After seven, on the other hand, all Dr. Happy had to do was walk through the service entrance to the laundry room, down a poorly lit hallway to the housekeeping break room, and he was sure to find Frank hunched over a wobbly folding table, playing cards with the custodial staff.

A hush fell over the formerly boisterous foursome seated around the table as Dr. Happy walked into the break room with silent confidence, approaching from behind Frank so that he couldn't see him enter. The other players peered over their cards at him quizzically, not sure if he was there to break up the party or if he was just lost. One thing they seemed to agree on: he did not give the impression that he was there to play poker. Frank, noting the change in mood and sensing Dr. Happy's presence behind him, turned around in his chair and looked up.

As soon as he saw Dr. Happy standing behind him, Frank smiled and turned back to the table. "No need to worry about him, boys." He fanned out the cards in his hand. "He's the biggest outlaw in here."

"Frank." Dr. Happy addressed him.

"Doc." Frank kept his attention square on his hand.

"I need a favor."

"Caught me in the middle of some business, doc." Frank winked at the other three card players.

"We have some real business to discuss, and I'm on the clock."

Frank turned back around to face Dr. Happy head on. "Excuse me? This *is* real business. That pot's got a lot of honey in it and I'm swimming with three legit sharks right here."

Dr. Happy decided to take another approach. "Hardly. These three couldn't look more out of their depth if they were emptying their bowels into their coveralls." Dr. Happy shot as sympathetic an expression as he could muster. "Gentlemen, I advise that you cut your losses now so Frank and I can have the table."

Three sets of cards fell onto the table, face down. After the amateurs silently shuffled out of the break room over his protests, Frank glared at Dr. Happy. "It took weeks for me to hook those fish."

Dr. Happy took one of the empty seats at the table. "Like I said. I'm on the clock."

Frank sighed. "Okay. But you can forget your preferred customer discount."


"Mr. McCann?"

Guy saw a gangly, unshaven man appear from the doors of one of the lobby elevators. Over a collared shirt he was wearing a white laboratory coat covered in coffee stains of different ages. The bags under his eyes and the way his shoulders hung told Guy he hadn't slept in his own bed for several days.

Guy nodded and the man in the dirty lab coat made a motioning gesture to Guy with the index and middle fingers of his right hand. Guy walked over to him and the man lowered his head toward Guy's.

"I'm the floor resident for the psychiatry service." He kept his voice to a whisper. "I need to tell you something that's rather...delicate in nature."

Guy felt a fluttering in his chest. Images of Blair being found on the floor of her hospital room bathroom, her wrists slashed open or overdosed on pills, raced through his mind. "What's going on?" His voice was much louder than the doctor's.

The doctor took a deep breath. "Ms. Weston eloped."

"Eloped?" Guy was left utterly confused. "You perform weddings here?"

"What?" The doctor made a face like Guy just said something stupid. "Oh, no," he said, a sudden realization to his voice. "No, Ms. Weston did not run off to get married."

"Okay," Guy said. "That's good...?"

"She just ran off," the doctor clarified. "Elopement is our euphemism for when a patient leaves the hospital against medical advice without telling anyone."

Guy felt his stomach drop. "I thought she was under an involuntary hold."

"She was." The doctor was talking so quietly that Guy could barely hear him.

"So, you mean you lost her?"

"Well, not exactly."

"But yesterday you had her," Guy stated.

"Correct."

"And today you don't."

"Unfortunately, no."

Guy's words came out slow and deliberate. "Well, not to get

technical with you, but that's exactly what it means to lose someone."

"Yeah...yes," the doctor stammered. "But..."

"How could this happen?" Guy's eyes were wide with anger. He could feel the hairs on his neck start to stand up.

"Right now, we don't know," the doctor answered. "It's a locked unit. There are security personnel on duty twenty-four hours a day."

Guy swallowed. "I imagine this happens very infrequently."

"Yes." Relief spread over the doctor's face. "*Very* infrequently."

Guy wrinkled his forehead and assessed the situation. "When it does happen, how is the person usually able to escape?" Guy could tell the doctor was on edge and switched his approach. "I'm not asking you how Blair escaped. I'm asking you: how is a person usually able to escape?"

The doctor took a pause.

"Just answer the question."

The doctor slowly spied over both shoulders, like he was about to tell a racist joke. "Usually it's a staffing error," he said. "The patient gets confused with someone else who has privileges to leave the unit."

"Or at least that's what they tell you."

"Excuse me?"

"I'm sure if a staff member were to *purposely* let a patient off the unit they weren't supposed to," Guy explained, "the easiest way for them to cover it up would be to say they mistook them for someone else."

The doctor's lips tightened in front of his clenched jaw. "What are you implying?"

"I'm sorry if I'm coming off as...accusatory." Guy let his shoulders relax for a second. "I've been up all night with nothing but convenience store coffee and bad synth pop music to keep me going. But you said you have security around the clock on the unit?"

"Yes."

"Guards, in other words?"

"Yes. Security guards."

"Men?"

"Excuse me?" The doctor seemed unsure of where Guy was going with this. He took a step backward, creating a few more inches distance between himself and Guy.

"Male guards," Guy clarified. "The security guards are usually men?"

"Most usually, yes."

"Can you tell me who was on guard last night?"

The doctor balked. "Look, I'm getting less and less comfortable having this conversation. I really have to get back to work." He started walking back to the elevator bay before turning back to Guy. "I'm sorry that Ms. Weston is gone, but we've already called the police to file a missing person report. There's very little we can do about it at this point. If you have concerns about how we're doing our job here, you can take it up with the hospital ombudsman."

Guy watched in disbelief as the doctor left. "Some hospital." He angrily called over to the girl at the information desk. "Does he really expect me to waste my time complaining to the hospital ombudsman?"

The girl twisted her mouth to the side for a second as if she were considering something, then offered Guy a muted smile. "His name is Frank," she said.

Guy was confused. "Oh, okay," he replied. "Does Frank really expect me to waste my time complaining to the hospital ombudsman?"

The girl's smile widened. "No, not the doctor."

Guy frowned. "The hospital ombudsman's name is Frank?"

The girl started laughing. "Stop it." She bit her lip to stop from giggling. "I mean the security guard."

Guy's hurried closer to the desk. "Excuse me?"

"I overheard you asking who the security guard for the psych unit was last night," she explained. "His name is Frank. I saw him come down from the twelfth floor this morning at change of shift."

Guy wet his lips with his tongue. "Do you know how I can find him?"

"When I saw him this morning, he told me he was going into a double shift," the girl answered. "So if you wander around the hospital long enough, you'll probably run into him."

"What does he look like?"

"Like a security guard. They all seem like they were sent from central casting. He looks the part, don't worry, and they all wear name tags," she said reassuringly. "You'll find him."

"Thanks," Guy said. As he turned from the desk, he noticed the torn blue comment card on the floor. He humbly picked up the pieces and placed them in front of the girl.

"Do you have another one of these I can fill out?"


Back in the break room, Dr. Happy was getting down to business. Frank secured his winnings in a brass money clip, clearly disappointed at the thinness of his wad.

"The way you so rudely interrupted my poker game," Frank began, "I presume that you have something in mind that is more worth my while?"

Dr. Happy nodded. "I need some PRBCs."

"Know the type?"

"Uh-uh. Better make it O negative."

"O neg's gonna cost, doc," Frank informed him. "Shortage going around. Thanks to Henry the fourth, they've had to destroy most the supply. And people are afraid to donate. Think they'll get infected just walking in here."

"Supply shock inflation." Dr. Happy handed him a roll of money.

"Ain't it a bitch," Frank said, pocketing the roll.

Satisfied with the advance payment, Frank led Dr. Happy

down a series of hallways. They were on the sub-basement level, far removed from the patient care traffic above.

"I assume this is for an associate," Frank said.

"Not of mine." Dr. Happy uncharacteristically allowed a bitter touch to his voice.

Frank gave a sympathetic nod. "They got you at beck and call, huh?"

Dr. Happy took in their surroundings. The exposed pipes and heavy chemical smells were the only features of the drab, unmarked hallway they walked down. "Not that different from working here, to be honest."

"Was he messed up bad?"

"Cut pretty deep. Needed lots of stitching. Had to babysit him most the night to make sure he didn't go into shock."

"Will he survive you taking this field trip?" Frank asked.

"Not my problem." Dr. Happy scratched at his jaw. "I was ordered to make this pickup. If he dies while I'm gone, that's not on me."

"Cold, man," Frank muttered, shaking his head. "Didn't you take an oath? *I will not cut for stone,* or something like that?"

"Yeah." Dr. Happy twisted his mouth. "*And may I enjoy my life and practice my art, respected by all humanity.*" He turned to Frank. "Do I look like I'm enjoying myself?"

Frank signaled for Dr. Happy to stop. "Wait here." Frank then disappeared through a set of double doors, the rear entrance to the blood bank.

A few minutes later, Frank returned carrying a Styrofoam cooler. He stood still, holding the cooler as Dr. Happy lifted the lid and inspected the contents.

"I'll also need some IV tubing and packing material," Dr. Happy said.

"I gotta talk to my boy in central supply, then. Here." Frank handed the cooler to Dr. Happy. "I'm late for my shift. I'm working a double covering the lobby. Go get a cup of coffee and I'll meet you there with the supplies."

Dr. Happy accepted the cooler and headed back down the hallway they had come from. He found his way to the main lobby from memory and spotted an empty table in a small atrium near the entrance. He pulled up a chair and slid the cooler under the table, scanning the lobby to make sure he hadn't raised any suspicions. He spotted Frank walking toward him ten minutes later, carrying a brown paper bag. Preparing for the delivery, Dr. Happy pulled the cooler a few inches out from under the table and lifted the lid.

Just as Frank approached the table, ready to toss the contents of the paper bag into the Styrofoam cooler, Dr. Happy spotted a tall, lanky man rushing over. Before either Dr. Happy or Frank could react, the man grabbed Frank by the arm and spun him around.

"Hey, asshole!" Guy McCann shouted, maintaining a tight grip on Frank's arm. "Do you have any idea what the legal consequences are for allowing a psychiatric inpatient to escape from a locked unit?"

Frank shot Guy a confused look and wrestled his arm free of his grip.

"What the hell are you talking about?" Frank's voice was restrained but forceful.

"What am I talking about?" Guy was growing red in the face. "Criminal negligence for starters. And if a single hair on her head is harmed outside this hospital, you're looking at full civil liability. That fat pension you've been looking forward to will end up being garnished for the rest of your life. Plus," Guy took a brief pause to catch his breath, "I am going to personally beat the shit out of you."

Frank took a step back, as if sizing Guy up. Frank easily had twenty pounds on him and a couple inches of reach.

"Be cool," Frank said. "I think maybe you have me confused with someone else."

"I don't think so, Frank." Guy pulled from his pocket the Polaroid of Blair he had taken from the hotel room and held it up. "Her name's Blair Weston. Look familiar? You're telling me you didn't intentionally let this woman out of the psych ward last night?"

"Wait." Dr. Happy stepped in and grabbed at the picture of Blair. He addressed Guy. "How do you know this girl?"

Guy turned away from Frank. "She's...wait..." He paused. His voice softened as he shot Dr. Happy a confused look. "How do *you* know her?"

Guy gave Dr. Happy a once over, trying to determine if his face rang any bells, but decided that wasn't the case. Then Guy noticed the open Styrofoam cooler and the bags of donor packed red blood cells inside.

"Who's all that blood for?" Guy asked.

"Why do you ask?" Dr. Happy responded.

A wave of realization swept over Guy, and he got the feeling that Dr. Happy was also putting two and two together. Neither of them moved as Guy stared him down.

Frank spoke in a low, deliberate tone. "All right," he began, "it seems like we all got something going on we don't feel like sharing right now." He paused and puffed out his chest. "However, *I'm* the only one who's wearing a badge. So I get to stay, and you two motherfuckers get to vacate the hell out of my hospital, right now."

Guy assessed Frank's height and weight, also noting the baton strapped to his belt. From the corner of his eye, he was keeping tabs on Dr. Happy, who seemed also to be appraising the situation.

Guy was the first to step back, arms up in a defensive pose. "Okay," he said. "My mistake." He took several steps backward, keeping his eyes on both Frank and Dr. Happy, before turning and briskly walking out the lobby entrance. Once he made it to the parking lot, Guy broke out into a dead sprint.

# CHAPTER 8

After scooping up the Styrofoam cooler, Dr. Happy had managed to run to the parking lot in time to see Guy hurry into his car. But once he saw the Datsun peel out into the street traffic, Dr. Happy lost interest in pursuing the matter any further. Like it or not, he was still on the clock and had a life to save.

By the time Dr. Happy returned to the hotel, his spine was aching from the weight of the Styrofoam cooler and the contents within. Rip's presence back in the hotel room had inspired such a rush to leave for the hospital that Dr. Happy hadn't thought to bring the hand cart with him. Already annoyed at his own carelessness, he was in no mood for the greeting he received upon entering the room.

"What's up, doc?" Rip cracked a sarcastic smile, opening the door just wide enough for Dr. Happy to squeeze through.

"We've been over this." Dr. Happy walked past him without making eye contact. "Doctors don't think that salutation is amusing."

"Really?" Rip's smile faded. "Well, what do piece-of-shit croaker quacks like you think about it?"

Dr. Happy considered his possible responses and the probable consequence of each. "We think it's hilarious."

Rip's smile returned. "That's more like it." He playfully slapped Dr. Happy on the cheek.

Dr. Happy recoiled in annoyance. Rather than reacting further, he silently regained his composure and turned his attention back to Bobby. He placed the Styrofoam cooler on the bed and pulled out one of the bags of donor blood along with the IV tubing. Carrying the blood, he walked past Rip into the bathroom and placed the bag in the sink, stopped the drain, and filled the basin with warm water.

"Any trouble?" Rip asked. He was now sitting in an armchair, playing with a red-handled stiletto switchblade, absently ejecting and retracting the blade. Dr. Happy imagined this was how he'd spent his last few hours.

Dr. Happy shook his head as he returned to Bobby's side, peeling back the blood-soaked gauze taped to Bobby's neck so he could inspect the wound.

"You sure?" Rip was studying the stiletto blade now, as if trying to figure out what to do with it next.

Dr. Happy opened a fresh package of gauze and changed Bobby's dressing. "If there had been any trouble, I wouldn't be here right now."

Rip's gaze lifted from his knife in response to Dr. Happy's derisive tone and his tongue reflexively darted to the corner of his mouth. Dr. Happy tried to focus on his tape job, but he could feel Rip's stare burning into the back of his head. Rip stood up from the chair and strode toward Dr. Happy, dragging the stiletto blade drag against the glass surface of the coffee table. The resulting screeching sound made Dr. Happy wince.

"And you didn't run into anyone suspicious?" Rip approached Dr. Happy's side and leaned in to his ear, his voice lowered to a whisper, "How did Bobby describe him? Tall, dark hair, big mouth?"

Dr. Happy shook his head again.

"Try hard to remember." Rip kept his mouth close to Dr. Happy, slowly exhaling warm breath onto Dr. Happy's ear with an exuberance that made his skin crawl. "Someone matching that description, looking for a girl, perhaps? Someone looking for that little cunt?" Distracted from his task, Dr. Happy took a step sideways away from Rip and turned to face him.

"No." Dr. Happy rubbed at his ear with his shoulder. "I didn't see anyone looking for Blair."

Small bubbles of saliva glistened along Rip's lips. He raised the stiletto, slowly drawing the point of the blade up toward Dr. Happy's chest. "Blair?"

Dr. Happy glanced down at the blade. "The girl from the Polaroids." He nodded toward the bedroom dresser where the stack of photographs sat. "The belle of the ballpark. The one who looks like she caught a case of the vapors."

"I never said her name was Blair." Rip's eyes seemed to be dancing in their sockets. "Who told you her name was Blair?"

The air tumbled out of Dr. Happy's lungs. No way to course correct at this point. He had to come clean or else he was going to be the one requiring a blood transfusion. Dr. Happy tried not to beat himself up too bad over the slip, telling himself that Rip probably smelled the guy on him when he came back to the hotel room anyway. "At the hospital," Dr. Happy answered. His eyes were still on the knife. "A tall guy, with dark hair."

"Big mouth?"

"You could say that."

"Looking for Blair?" Rip asked with genuine interest, although still holding the knife directly in front of Dr. Happy's heart. "Why at the hospital?"

Dr. Happy's eyes rose to meet Rip's and found himself looking into an empty gaze, two eyes, dark like a doll's. "I think she had been in the psych unit," he answered. "But it sounds like she escaped."

Rip pressed the tip of the blade against Dr. Happy's chest. "Well, that sounds like pertinent information, doctor." He started slowly rolling the stiletto handle in his hand so that the tip of the blade made a screwing motion into Dr. Happy's chest. "Escaped to where?"

"Whereabouts unknown," Dr. Happy answered automatically.

"I see," Rip replied. "Is there anything else about this mystery gentleman?"

Dr. Happy motioned toward Bobby. "The blood is probably warm enough by now," he said. "I should go start the transfusion."

Rip ignored him, keeping the blade's tip pressed against Dr. Happy. "Anything else?" He increased the pressure on the blade, pushing the tip through the fabric of Dr. Happy's shirt. A small red pinpoint formed on his shirt as the blade punctured the surface of the skin underneath.

"I should go start the transfusion, Rip," Dr. Happy repeated. "Otherwise Bobby could die."

Rip's gaze rose from Dr. Happy's chest to meet his eyes. Gripping the handle of the switchblade tightly, he swung out viciously to his side, slicing through the IV tubing that was delivering the saline solution to Bobby's bloodstream. Saline poured onto the bed as Dr. Happy stood frozen in place. Rip's expression remained as serene as it was when he was giving himself the manicure just moments ago.

*He's about to kill me, and his heart rate is barely sixty beats per minute.*

"Anything else?" Rip asked. His voice was so quiet Dr. Happy could barely hear him.

Dr. Happy swallowed to make sure his throat was lubricated enough for his vocal cords to work properly. "His car."

"You saw what he was driving?"

"He got into a red Z. Not this year's model though. Looks like it had some mileage."

Hearing this information seemed to set Rip on fire. "Motherfucker!" he exclaimed, his cheeks flushing crimson. He gnashed his teeth and turned away from Dr. Happy, holding the knife in an offensive pose as if ready to square off with an invisible combatant. "Tall, dark hair, big mouth," he fumed. "That son of a bitch."

He charged over to the bed and slapped Bobby across his

unconscious face. "You didn't mention limp-dicked and rat-faced!" he shouted. "If you had, we might have saved ourselves some time!"

Dr. Happy watched cautiously in silence. After pacing the room for several minutes, Rip's rage dissipated and a wild-eyed smile formed on his face. Taking a deep breath, he walked over to the telephone on the nightstand and dialed.

"Mickey?" Rip said crisply into the receiver. "It looks like Prince fucking Charming just rode back into town. He's apparently looking for the little cunt. So I'm going to need you to find him before he finds her."

Dr. Happy remained glued in place. He knew that conversations like this took place, but this was the first time he had ever overheard one.

"Start with the hooker motels near the hospital," Rip instructed into the phone. "That degenerate shouldn't be able to float more than five bucks a night for where he flops. And bring him back here. Alive." He paused for a moment and considered. "But not necessarily in one piece," Rip added. "Feel free to break any bone in his body except his jaw. I need that big mouth of his in working condition so that if he knows where Blair is, I'm able to get it out of him."

He paused to listen to the reply from the other end of the phone.

"Do I think I'll get him to talk?" Rip asked. "I'm going to get him to sing me a fucking rock opera." With his free hand, he lifted the stiletto and held the edge of the blade up to his gaze. "Then I'm going to cut out his goddamn soul."

# CHAPTER 9—December 7, 1985

"You have nothing to worry about," Guy McCann said, trying to sound trustworthy. "My guess is that the prosecution is bluffing."

"Your guess? I'm not paying you to guess."

"You're not paying me to look good either," Guy said. "But here it is all the same."

Sitting across from Guy was Eugene Cusatis, referred to by his friends and the newspapers as Geno the Nose. Cusatis raised an eyebrow and scratched at the edge of his pencil thin mustache with his fingernail. He did not appear convinced.

Guy relaxed his smile a touch and met his client's dark, unforgiving eyes, making sure his gaze didn't linger on Cusatis's prominent beak. "All they have is circumstantial evidence," he began. "Thanks to your rather creative bookkeeping, they don't have any material evidence of any kickbacks. And like you said, it's not against the law for your wife to own a trucking company. Even if she doesn't know the first thing about driving a truck."

Cusatis nodded silently in agreement. The rest of his broad frame, barely contained by his dark double-breasted suit, remained immobile.

"The feds don't want to be embarrassed by losing this in court," Guy went on. "They know their only chance at a conviction is if you plea down. If we hold our ground and show them we're willing to take this to trial, then I guarantee they drop the charges."

"You guarantee?" Cusatis barked, his eyes wide with indignation. "Easy for you to say. You're not the one looking at five to ten on Terminal Island."

"Losing this trial doesn't do me any favors," Guy said. "In this town, a lawyer's reputation is all he's got. I don't make a lay-up like this, word gets out that I don't know a sidebar from a salad bar, and next thing you know I'm trading in my S-Class for a Gremlin."

Cusatis grinned in spite of himself. "All right." He slammed a massive palm onto the table. "You have my trust. Don't misuse it."

"Not in the cards," Guy assured him.

Cusatis rose and shook Guy's hand with an intensity that managed to exude both warmth and intimidation. As soon as Cusatis exited and the door had closed behind him, Milloy rose from his chair in the corner and approached Guy with a knowing smile.

"Laying it on a little thick, aren't you, Counselor?" he asked. "Since when do you drive an S-Class?"

"Soon as I cash his check."

"Careful, McCann," Milloy warned him. "I'm not sure that delicate frame of yours can support the weight if your head gets any bigger."

Guy frowned. "It's hard not to get cocky when all I'm getting are these cookie-cutter union-bust witch-hunt cases. Defending the Local Brotherhood of Piecutters 101." Guy ran his hand through his hair and furrowed his eyebrows. "I don't know where these federal prosecutors went to law school, but they must have taken the short bus to get there. Take that last case I tried. Lead prosecution pointed out during closing that my client didn't take the stand. Automatic mistrial. And these indictments are so half baked, it's like they're trying to lose in court."

Milloy took a sip from the glass he was holding. After clearing his throat, he turned back to Guy. "I've got news."

"Good or bad?"

Milloy paused. "Good." He walked over to the side of the room where Guy was standing and forced a smile. "Great, actually. Casparo wants to meet you."

Guy stood stunned. For a rare moment, he was speechless.

"Where?" he blurted out once the moment passed, almost stuttering. "When...I mean, why?"

"His house." Milloy then added: "Tonight." And then: "Because he likes what he's seen." He took another sip of his drink. "These cookie-cutter cases...not that they've been a test. But if they were, let's just say that you passed. He's got something he wants to bring you in on."

"Why didn't he ask you?" he asked with a hesitant tone.

"I don't know," Milloy replied. "He didn't say, so I didn't ask." He then added, good-naturedly: "Don't worry, I'm not threatened. There's plenty of pie to be sliced here." Then, almost as an afterthought: "Trust me."


The car drove Guy and Milloy to a plantation-style mansion in Beverly Hills, through a heavy iron gate and up a long driveway that led to the house. As they approached, Milloy caught Guy peering out the window, studying the scene carefully.

"What are you doing?" he asked.

"Looking for snipers on the roof," Guy answered without looking away from the window.

"I don't think he's that paranoid," Milloy replied.

The car pulled to the front of the house and the two men exited, climbing a small flight of stone steps to the door. Upon their arrival to the threshold, the main door opened and they were greeted by two men, each wearing expensive suits and blank expressions. One of them, the darker of the two, took a hold of Guy at his elbow, sending an involuntary shiver down his back. The man then guided Guy in the direction of the main hallway and turned, releasing Guy's elbow and swiveling away in a manner such that as he turned, his sport coat fell open just enough to allow Guy a view of the .38 caliber pistol holstered against his left flank. Guy had the impression this had been intentional.

The armed man led Guy and Milloy through a marble foyer, down a long hallway, and through a pair of French doors that opened into an office at the rear of the house. Inside the office, a window faced a swimming pool and an expansive topiary garden. In front of the window sat a large custom oak desk, meticulously carved and treated. And seated at the desk was Antonin Casparo.

He looked Guy over. Whether he was impressed or disappointed with what he saw, his chiseled and weather-beaten countenance gave no indication. Guy stood anxiously before him, Milloy standing silently to his left.

"I've been following your caseload," Casparo began. His voice was the sound of something being dragged over gravel. "Your record is quite commendable."

"I can't take too much credit," Guy said with a wink. "It's not so hard when you're defending the innocent."

Casparo produced a wet, choking laugh from deep in his throat. "Yes, of course." He offered a charitable smile. "Well, I've asked you here because I'd like to you to take on a case as a favor to me."

Guy's heart rate increased in response but he kept silent.

"I do hope it won't tarnish your winning streak," Casparo continued. "More innocents to defend, I should say."

"Of course." Guy returned Casparo's deliberate grin.

"You may have heard about a little trouble that occurred about a year ago in Hollywood. A few girls were arrested for solicitation inside a nightclub."

The well-tanned armed man who had escorted Guy and Milloy to the office walked over and handed a dossier to Guy.

"The papers are calling them the Sunset Seven," Casparo

continued. "They are finally getting their day in court, and I am not confident in the competence of their current counsel."

Guy glanced at the brief he had just been handed. "What is your interest in the case?" he asked.

"An actor was involved," Casparo replied. "That's the only reason the girls were even charged. Otherwise this would have been swept under the rug much more discreetly. But you know how the press gets when they are handed a story that they can turn into something salacious. It's become a bit of an embarrassment. I happen to own the nightclub and the actor involved is a close friend of the family."

"I imagine that if they avoid conviction then this story will go away a lot faster."

"Precisely," Casparo replied. "If you could simply explain to the jury that this was all just a misunderstanding."

"Of course," Guy assured him.

Back in the car, Guy was glowing like he just got asked to prom by the captain of the football team. Milloy meanwhile was looking at him with consternation. Guy turned toward him and raised an eyebrow.

"Something on your mind?" Guy asked playfully.

Milloy answered by casting his eyes in the direction of the well-tanned gunman, who was sitting across from them in the back of the Town Car.

"Don't wear out that game show host smile on the car ride home," Milloy warned, a hint of derision in his tone. "You'll need it for the jury box when you go to trial."

Guy frowned. "Any other advice?" he asked, down-shifting the level of excitement in his voice.

"Don't expect a fee," Milloy answered. "You won't get one."

"What?" Guy nearly fell out of his seat. "Then what's the point?"

"What you will get is access to Casparo," Milloy continued.

"And that access you are free to sell." Milloy's voice suddenly became rote, as if he were giving driving directions. "For example, don't be surprised if you start getting calls from land developers looking for a pension fund loan. If you think the investment seems reasonable, Casparo is likely to provide that loan. And you are well within your legal rights to collect a finder's fee for securing the developer with that loan."

Guy glanced at the gunman across from them. If he had any objection to their conversation, or was even paying attention, his expression didn't show it.

The car pulled up in front of Guy's apartment complex. As he turned to climb out, Milloy grabbed at his coat sleeve.

"That brief," Milloy said, motioning to the dossier Casparo handed Guy earlier. "Make sure you look at it right away."

Guy laughed. "Why are you so serious all of a sudden? They don't expect me to start working on this until tomorrow. Tonight I'm going to celebrate."

Not waiting for a response, Guy stepped out of the car and onto the sidewalk. But before he could head up the path to his apartment, Guy heard a voice that didn't belong to Milloy call to him.

"Hey Counselor," the voice said. Guy turned and saw that it was the hitherto silent gunman, beckoning to him with a subtle but eerie grin.

"*In bocca al lupo*," the gunman said softly.

Guy just stood there silently, his perplexed expression contorting his face. The gunman's grin stretched into a leering smile and his tongue darted to the corner of his mouth. Then the car sped off from the curb, leaving Guy alone on the sidewalk, looking clueless.


After a few moments, Guy shook off the awkward encounter and rushed into his apartment, where he hurriedly showered, shaved, Stetsoned, and Studio Lined. Within the hour he was walking back into the nightclub where he and Milloy had celebrated his passing the bar. Compelled by a gravitational force, Guy walked briskly into the dining room and found her standing near the bar. She was alone.

Guy approached her without hesitation, though he worried at the last moment that she might not recognize him. As he neared her, she took notice of him and smiled in a way that was so automatic Guy couldn't tell if it was a genuine reaction to their reunion or a rehearsed response to male attention.

And then Blair said: "Have you come back to check my mileage?"

Guy beamed, then checked himself, trying to remain nonchalant. "I'm over the sticker shock, if that's what you mean," he replied. "I'm here to buy you a drink."

Blair's eyebrows rose in response. She took a half step backward, opening up a space between Guy and the bar. "Then by all means."

Guy approached the bartender with resolve. "Two glasses of that fifteen-year Macallan, neat."

"And a bib for the gentleman," Blair added.

"The bib won't be necessary," Guy informed the bartender. He then added: "But maybe a water back just in case." He turned to Blair. "At least I made an impression with you."

"That you did."

The bartender returned with the drinks and Guy escorted Blair to a small table near the back of the dining room.

"May I ask you a question?" he asked a few minutes later after working up the nerve to break free of the small talk they had settled into.

"You may." She took on a suspicious tone.

"The night we met," Guy said, "it seemed like you were in a row with Anneleise Casparo. What was it about?"

Blair lifted her glass to her lips and then paused. "I wouldn't let her copy my algebra homework," she said, before taking a sip.

"In other words, it's none of my business."

"In other words," Blair lifted her eyebrows and leaned in toward Guy, "there are much better things we could be doing together than discussing that unfortunate event."

"Anything come to mind?"

Blair simply smiled in response.

When the waiter returned and refreshed their drinks, Guy caught him taking a lingering glance at Blair. He was young, probably putting himself through college. Guy intended to keep this observation to himself. However, when he turned his attention from the waiter's leering eye back to Blair, she was giving him a knowing look.

"He must be new," Blair surmised. Her tone was neutral. She appeared neither offended nor flattered by the waiter's attention. "Charlie would throw him out on his ear if he caught him eyeing the guests that way."

"He probably couldn't help himself," Guy said with a grin. "I'd wager you have a knack for causing men to make bad decisions."

Blair let the last comment drift. "But why do men do that, I wonder," she mused. "Stare like we can't tell we're being stared at. Call me crazy, but doesn't it strike you as a bit rude?"

"You're crazy," Guy replied. "And you don't have to look at it necessarily as being rude."

"Then how should I look at it?"

Guy thought for a moment then sat up straight in his chair, a twinkle appearing in his eye. "Have you ever been to a museum?" He took a formal tone, as if cross-examining her.

"Yes." The fingers of both her hands tapped gently along the length of her glass.

"Did you just walk down the hall with your eyes straight ahead," Guy asked, "or did you stop to appreciate the beauty that was all around you?"

Blair sat back in her chair, putting more distance between herself and Guy, but with a playful air. "Women are not works of art, Counselor."

"Not all of them." Guy reached across the table and placed his hand over hers. His cocky tenor relaxed into one of sincerity and he gazed into her eyes as he repeated: "Not all of them."

"I walked right into that one, didn't I?" Blair asked.

Guy leaned back in his chair and rested his hands in front of him, his fingers crossed. "You tell me," he replied. "Have I taken my eyes off of you since I've been here?"

"Only to look in the mirror behind the bar."

"I think that proves my point."

"So," Blair said. "The defense rests its case?"

Guy lifted his glass to his lips and drained the remaining liquid into his mouth. "The verdict?" he asked.

Blair sat silently for a few seconds, closing and opening her eyelashes, as if in a state of careful consideration. Finally, she responded: "The jury needs time to deliberate. I think a sequestration is in order."

Guy felt his jaw fall open. "Should I ask for the check?" His voice was close to stammering.

"No." Blair rose from her chair and extended her arm to him. "It'll go on your tab."

"When did I start running a tab?" Guy asked as he followed Blair toward the ballroom exit.

His heart was beating so intensely that he could feel his pulse in his ears. This made it difficult to hear Blair when she answered, just above a whisper: "The moment you stepped into the bar."


When Guy awoke, he was alone in bed. He sat up and scanned the room anxiously, a bit unnerved that Blair had departed. Her outline was still visible on the pillow next to his. There, occupying her place in the bed, was a piece of legal pad paper with a phone number written on it. Guy picked it up and held it close to his face. Underneath the phone number were written the words:

*Call me,*
*Crazy*

Guy smiled and held the note tightly, rubbing his thumb over the handwriting as if to make sure it was real and not a hallucination. After a few moments of this, he rose, threw on an old college sweatshirt and a pair of workout pants, and put a pot of coffee on to brew. He then sat down at the kitchen table, where he had left the dossier that Casparo's body man had handed him the evening before.

Guy opened the dossier and pulled out several bound sheets of legal documents from inside. He flattened them on the table, his mind still wandering back to his evening with Blair. He rubbed the sleep from his eyes and tried to push her image temporarily out of his mind, his desire to impress Casparo shifting him into work mode.

Then he froze. As the aroma of his gourmet medium blend filled the room, Guy felt the joy of the previous evening being sucked out of him. On top of the stack of legal briefs was a list naming the indicted women who made up the Sunset Seven. The seven women who were now his clients.

Among them was Blair Weston.

Guy frantically sifted through the briefs, his heart racing and eyes darting about the pages. He found a stack of booking paperwork among the police records, containing the fingerprints and mug shots of the seven women accused of solicitation. Guy pulled one of the six-by-eight glossy black and white prints from the stack. Blair's face was unmistakable. She was looking up at Guy from the picture with the same demure gaze that she had showed him when they met the night before at the nightclub. She was even flashing the same rehearsed smile.

Guy didn't react to the coffee maker's alarm or the pungent smell of burnt coffee filling the kitchen. He just sat at the table, unable to move.

# CHAPTER 10—September 30, 1987

Guy was starting to have trouble focusing his eyes. He had come to the bar to think, to figure out what to make of the man with the cooler full of blood and a working knowledge of Blair's appearance. What had driven Blair to the psychiatric unit and what had compelled her to break out less than twenty-four hours later? He had come to the bar to exercise his mind but had ended up working out his drinking elbow instead. When the bartender finally suggested, rather aggressively, that he had occupied his barstool long enough, Guy wasn't in any shape to do much else but nod dumbly, toss a couple bills on the counter, and shuffle out to his car. After several failed attempts to insert key into ignition, Guy managed to put the Z in drive and tried to find his way back to his motel.

After parking across two spots in the lot, Guy exited his car and climbed the concrete steps leading to the second-floor hallway. At the top of the stairs sat a lean, reptilian man in a metal folding chair. He wore a splayed collared shirt, unbuttoned from neck to navel, and a black fedora tilted forward over his eyes.

"Hey, man," he said, noticing Guy coming up the stairs. "You ready for some action tonight?"

"Already told you," Guy answered. "Not in the market."

"You'll change your mind soon," the pimp replied. "And

when you do, don't worry. We're always open for business."

Guy walked past him, repulsed by the offer. But he paused after a few steps, thinking the pimp might have some utility after all. "Hey," Guy said, turning back around, "has anyone been to my room?"

The pimp leaned back and tipped up his hat to get a better look at Guy. "Say they have?" he asked. "How much is that information worth?"

Guy pulled a ten-dollar bill from his pocket and walked back toward the pimp, holding the bill out for him to see.

"Only a sawbuck?"

Guy shrugged. "It's all I got."

The pimp let out a condescending laugh and snatched the ten spot from Guy's grip.

"No, man," he crooned, gold-capped teeth catching the light of the late afternoon sun. "No one's been by. You all right."

"*I all right*?" Guy was not entirely satisfied with the transaction. "No one's been by my room? No one's come by asking about me?"

"I said you all right," the pimp reassured him.

"And you'd know, right?" Guy asked.

"Been sitting here all day." The pimp pointed to his chair. "So I'd know."

Guy shook his head and stumbled down the hall to his motel room. Once he got to the door to his room, he pulled the key from his pocket and began the struggle of threading it into the lock.

"Not for nothing," Guy said loudly over his shoulder, directing his voice to the pimp down the hall, "but I'm a little dubious about the validity of your claim. If the quality of the ladies in your employ is as suspect as the information you're selling, you can forget any ideas about my future patronage." He finally managed to get the key in the lock. "Besides," he added, "when I'm this drunk, I'm only good for one thing…"

The door swung open and Guy found himself staring face-to-face with a broad-shouldered man holding a .357 Magnum.

"...getting into trouble," Guy finished.

The owner of the .357 smiled at Guy. "Hello, Counselor."

Guy turned back toward the pimp, who offered a sheepish shrug.

"Sorry, man." He was still sitting back casually in his lawn chair. "He paid me twenty to keep my mouth shut. You look like a nice guy. I was going to warn you if you matched his offer."

The thug approached Guy. "You picked a bad time to turn cheapskate."

"Hardly," Guy replied. "Whatever you have planned, I'm so tanked up right now I doubt I'll feel a thing. So I'd say my timing was impeccable."

"We'll see." The thug kept the .357 pointed at Guy's chest.

Guy was staring so intently at the gun that he didn't notice the right hook until it made contact with his temple, and then only for a second before everything went black.

# CHAPTER 11

Bobby had regained consciousness and was asking for something to eat. The color was still drained from his skin, and his lips were pale and chapped. This did not, however, prevent him from using his mouth. "Get me the goddamn room service menu," he kept barking at Dr. Happy. "I'm sick of just laying around staring at the goddamn ceiling."

"You can have clear liquids to start with." Dr. Happy handed him a glass of water. "But bear in mind that your condition, while stable at the moment, is still serious. Start low and go slow."

"Start low and go slow?" Bobby parroted. "You trying to get me to fellate you?" He knocked the glass out of Dr. Happy's hand with the back of his fist. "And what's with this kid glove shit? I've been lying on this bed for a day and a half. Give me a goddamn real drink, will you?"

"I advise you start with water," Dr. Happy answered. "You need hydration. You were briefly in hypovolemic shock, and I'm not sure your GI tract will be able to handle anything more than that."

"With all the blood he lost, you ought to be stuffing him full of filet mignon," Rip's voice interjected from the anteroom.

Dr. Happy's molars ground against each other as Rip entered the bedroom. Rip's toothy grin had been an unavoidable fixture in the hotel room since he got off the phone with Mickey. Dr.

Happy had been growing tired of Rip's frenetic energy and was running out of ways to keep himself from saying so.

"We're paying you to sew him up." Rip continued his walk toward Dr. Happy. "Not to be his wet nurse."

Dr. Happy held out his arms in mock surrender, the gesture also serving to keep Rip from encroaching Dr. Happy's personal space any further. "You're both adults." Dr. Happy tried to avoid sounding sarcastic. "I'm not going to stop you from ordering room service. But I'm not going to make the call for you either."

The telephone was on the nightstand, just out of Bobby's reach. Groaning, he strained to sit himself up in the bed. After much effort, he found himself at the edge of the bed, legs dangling limp over the side of the mattress, breathing heavily.

"There, you happy?" Bobby panted. "Didn't even bust a stitch, I don't think. Now hand me the goddamn phone."

Before Dr. Happy could respond, the door burst open and a heavyset man entered the hotel room. A second man, leaner and semi-conscious, was hanging from around his shoulder. Dr. Happy immediately recognized the second man from the hospital lobby. The rapidly swelling bruise under his left eye was a new addition.

"Is that him?" Rip asked. Dr. Happy could swear he saw Rip's pupils dilate as he watched Mickey carry the man into the hotel room.

"Yeah," Mickey replied. "I found him in a working joint near the hospital. Just like you said."

That toothy grin of Rip's widened. "Get him in here," he said, motioning Bobby into the bedroom. "I want to get a look at him."

Mickey dragged Guy across the sitting room and Rip hurried to close the door behind them.

"Did anyone see you coming up?" Rip asked, following Mickey toward the bedroom.

Mickey shook his head. "I took the loading entrance around back. No one was around. They have a separate elevator that comes up down the far end of the hall by the laundry."

Rip guided Mickey into the bedroom. "Here, get him in the chair."

Mickey unloaded Guy into an armchair in the corner of the hotel bedroom. Dr. Happy glanced silently over Mickey's shoulder to get a look at the payload. Guy was awake but appeared concussed. His eyes were struggling to converge and he had the slack stare of a punch-drunk boxer. Rip approached the chair with a bounce in his step that bordered on giddiness. He lightly slapped Guy's face.

"Hey," Rip whispered. "Baby boy. Wake up, baby boy."

Guy stirred. He let out a dull moan and his eyelids fluttered. Rip was standing right in front of him when Guy's eyes fully opened, and Guy bolted upright, recoiling back into the chair in terror. Rip was licking his lips, as if to keep from drooling on himself.

"It's time to take your medicine." Rip swung his right fist into Guy's face, catching Guy right above his left eye with the power and precision of an experienced prizefighter. Guy's head whipped back, then fell forward as his body went limp.

Dr. Happy took a small step backward. "I thought you wanted to make him talk," he said to Rip. "Not beat him to a pulp."

Rip turned back to face him. "Let's not rush things," he replied. "And be sure, I intend to do both." He turned to Mickey and then motioned to the ice bucket that sat on one of the hotel towels on top of the bedroom dresser. "Is that full?"

Mickey peered into the bucket and nodded. Rip motioned for Mickey to bring it to him. With both hands Rip took the bucket, three-quarters full of ice and water, and threw the contents into Guy's face. The shock jolted Guy awake, and he sputtered and twisted his head from side to side. He took a deep gasp and opened his eyes again.

"Wha-what? Wha-what?" he kept repeating over and over, looking around the room as if he couldn't believe he was really there and that this was really happening.

Rip cupped a hand under Guy's chin, like a mother would when consoling her child, and raised his head up to face Rip's.

"Welcome back to the coast, barrister," Rip said. "I'm sorry if your homecoming party isn't as *chic* as you had envisioned. It's the best we could put together on such short notice."

"Wha-what," Guy stuttered. His teeth were chattering. "What do you want?"

"What do I want?" Rip asked. "That's a little insulting. I'm sure you have quite a strong grasp on what I want." He let go of Guy's chin and passed his hand over Guy's face, gently sliding it up to his hairline and brushing back Guy's forelock in a motion that resembled a lover's caress, until he grabbed a fistful of Guy's hair and pulled, jerking his head backward so forcefully it practically snapped off. "You've been derelict in your duties, Counselor. And that leaves you with a lot of explaining to do. In fact, it wouldn't be out of line if I opened you like an Angus steer right now to make up for lost time." Rip tossed Guy's head to the side and stood over him, taking a deep breath. "But I'm afraid that's going to have to wait a little longer. I know that little cunt of yours has been sniffing around the boss's business, and now she's disappeared."

"I haven't seen her," Guy said in choking gasps.

"Haven't seen who?" Rip barked back.

"Blair."

"Bullshit," Rip snapped. "The cunt packs shop and makes like vapor, and by coincidence, suddenly you show up back in town. Unannounced. In her hotel room."

"I haven't seen her," Guy repeated. "That's the truth."

"Oh, is that the truth?" Rip snapped.

It took all the energy Guy had to move his head up and down in the affirmative.

"The whole truth?" His voice took on a mocking air of authority.

"Yes," Guy replied.

"And nothing but the...dot, dot, dot?" Rip's fingers punctuated the last three syllables.

Guy's words came out in panting breaths: "So...help...me...G—"

His words were interrupted by Rip's fist swinging into his jaw. Guy's head violently whipped to the side with the blow. Rip pulled himself back up and peered down at Guy.

"*I'm* the only one who can help you now," Rip said. "And I'm giving you the chance to come clean without me having to beat it out of you."

Guy sputtered at him: "Rip, wait." His voice was pleading. "Let's talk this through. Let me tell you what I can bring to the table. Let's discuss this like professionals."

"Are you trying to negotiate?" Rips asked. "I forgot how big a ball buster you were, Counselor." Rip knelt down so the two were eye to eye. "I know that your head's probably spinning right now, and you're still trying to make sense of what's going on. So I'm going to spell it all out for you. You are going to die in this hotel room. How long it takes, and how much pain I get to inflict upon you, those are the only things on the table. That's all you get to negotiate."

Guy held his hands out in a defensive pose. "I don't know where she is," he said. "My hand to God. But maybe we can still work something out."

"I think I know what you're trying to pull," Rip said. "I think that you think that if you keep stalling with your bullshit, that eventually the cops are going to bust through the door and save you. You're willing to take the taps to the head to buy yourself time. You figure that someone must have seen Mickey drag you up here. Someone must have heard me thumping on you by now and gotten suspicious enough to drop the dime."

Rip dropped his arms to his sides in resignation. He casually walked to the dresser against the wall and leaned against it. "You remind me of my little brother Oscar," Rip continued. "He always thought he knew all the angles too. A real smart fucker." Rip absently drummed his fingertips against the top of the dresser. "Take this one summer when we were kids, for example. It's a hot day in July and me and some of my cousins want to have a water balloon fight. You know, little kid shit. So we pull Oscar outside to play with us. And even though he's a scrawny runt at the time, and even though he knows I'm just asking him so I have an excuse to tag the little fucker, Oscar smiles and says okay.

"So we're out in the neighborhood, tossing balloons at each other, running from each other, all that happy shit, when suddenly I catch Oscar all defenseless up against a fence. He's used up all his balloons—*he's empty-handed*—so I know I really got the little bastard. So, I take my water balloon and I hold it out in front of him, taunting him, you know. Letting him know I really mean to give it to him. And Oscar, the smart little fucker, he just gives me this look. No fear, no regard. Just this fucking look like he was saying, *Go ahead motherfucker, give it your best shot.*

"So I take that water balloon and I toss it as hard as I can, and wouldn't I be great goddamned but I nail the fucker right in the *coglioni*. Right in the fucking balls. Couldn't have made that toss again if I had a hundred tries. The balloon hits his little pencil dick like a fucking bullseye. And you could hear it snap on impact—*bam!*—from a mile away. And Oscar. Holy shit. He grabs his balls like they just got blown clean off. He starts wailing like a stuck bitch. The whole fucking neighborhood heard it. Old ladies are sticking their heads out the windows yelling like they think someone just got shot. And I know with all the fucking screaming he's doing and all the commotion he's causing, it's only a matter of time before my old man gets wise. So I run over and I start yelling at him, shut up you stupid runt, it's not that bad. You're going to get me in dutch with the old man.

"And wouldn't you know it, but my old man comes out, hearing Oscar screaming bloody murder and lying on the street like he's been stabbed. And he sees me hovering over him with this sick, guilty look on my face. He doesn't have to think twice about it before he balls one up and *pow!* Had me seeing stars. Later on, when I'm sitting in my room with a pack of frozen peas on my face, I ask Oscar, how come you had to be such a pussy about it? Didn't you know the old man was going to hide me if you didn't shut up with that shit? Didn't you know all your crying was going to get me coldcocked? Oscar just looks up at me and smiles and says, *Of course, you stupid fuck. Why do you think I agreed to the water balloon fight to begin with?*"

Rip walked back over to Guy's chair, eyes narrowed to a squint like he was making sure Guy had been paying attention. "See," Rip continued, "I think you're thinking like my brother Oscar. You don't mind taking a blow to the nuts if it means getting to watch me get clobbered. But the difference is, unlike my brother, there's no one here who gives a shit if they find *you* lying on the street, screaming bloody murder. My old man gave a shit about Oscar, that's why he knocked my block off. But, no one's coming to save you, Counselor. Because no one gives a shit about you."

Guy took several deliberate, deep breaths, then slowly stood up. His knees started buckling but he was able to keep upright. He took a single, unsteady step toward Rip and then stopped. "Rip," he began.

Guy was interrupted by Rip's fist slamming into his stomach, doubling him over so that he fell forward into Rip. Guy wrapped his arms around Rip as he tried to keep on his feet. Disgusted, Rip pushed Guy back into the chair. Guy grabbed his abdomen and bent forward, coughing up large globs of bloody saliva.

"Last chance, Romeo." Rip pulled the stiletto from his pocket and flipped open the blade. "Tell me where I can find your cunt girlfriend, or I'm going to use your insides to turn this hotel room into a modern art gallery."

Guy closed his eyes, leaned forward, and vomited onto the carpeted floor. Rip took a step backward as his face twisted into a revolted scowl. Guy spat onto the floor, trying to clear the blood-tinged discharge from his mouth. He strained to raise his head, his lids hanging heavy over bloodshot eyes. "I can't help you, Rip," he said. "And even if I could, you know I wouldn't."

"And they say chivalry is dead," Rip said. "Well, in your case, they're right." He peered down at the puddle of vomit on the carpet and winced. "You really know how to kill the mood, Counselor. I try to create a certain dramatic tension with that little speech of mine, and you follow it up by puking all over the floor." Rip closed his knife and returned it to his pocket before straightening himself up and turning to Mickey. "We've wasted enough time on this scumbag. If Casanova won't tell me the secrets he's keeping in his head, then we're just going to have to set them free, all over the goddamn walls."

Mickey pulled the Magnum out from under his jacket and pointed it at Guy.

Rip's smile returned. "In the face," he ordered. "I want to permanently erase that asshole's shit-eating grin from existence."

Unable to help himself, Dr. Happy let out an audible sigh from the corner of the room.

Rip's smile faded. He turned to Dr. Happy with a look of contempt. "What?" he asked.

Dr. Happy shook his head. "You already had me turn this place into a MASH unit. Now you want to paint the walls with this guy's brains? Is the term *low profile* a completely foreign concept to you?" He pointed to Mickey's gun. "The blast from that .357 is over 160 decibels. You shoot him with that, every hotel guest, chambermaid, and bellboy five floors above and below will hear it. There are only about a hundred other ways to kill him that would draw less attention."

"Oh?" Rip said. "A hundred other ways that would draw less attention?" He took a step closer to Dr. Happy and raised his eyebrows in a feigned look of interest. "Is that something you learned in medical school?"

"No, Rip," Dr. Happy countered. "It's something I learned

in *obvious* school."

The words hung over the room for a moment as Rip stared at Dr. Happy, his eyes returning to their cold, expressionless form. Mickey and Bobby exchanged glances, like they were both wondering if they'd be disposing of two bodies instead of just one. But then Rip took a deep breath and regained his composure. "All right, Doctor," he said. "In your professional opinion, what would you suggest?"

Dr. Happy reached for his black bag. "Let me give him a hot dose," he answered. "The cops find him OD'd in his old girlfriend's hotel room right after she went AWOL from the psych ward, they won't break their necks looking for any leads past that."

Rip stood silent for a moment, his gaze fixed on Dr. Happy. He then suddenly let out a laugh and condescendingly slapped Dr. Happy on the cheek. "Yours truly is a noble profession." He turned to Mickey. "All right, get him on the bed so the good doctor can get to work."

Mickey grabbed Guy and dragged him out of the chair onto the bed. Bobby, who had up until this point been contently watching the action from the edge of the bed, was now forced out of the way. He tried to rise to his feet with his own strength, but found his legs go weak once he stood up. Noticing this, Dr. Happy glanced at Rip and nodded in Bobby's direction. Visibly unhappy with receiving an order—albeit a discreet, nonverbal one—instead of giving one, Rip scowled and pushed Bobby back so he was leaning up against the nightstand next to the bed instead of in danger of falling to the floor. Rip then turned his attention back to Mickey, who had used his considerable weight advantage to pin Guy to the mattress. While Guy tried feebly to break free from Mickey's grip, Dr. Happy pulled a prefilled syringe out of his bag. He inspected the yellow tape wrapped around the cylinder and attached a twenty-two-gauge hypodermic needle to the tip.

"I'm ready," Dr. Happy said. "Hold down his arm."

Guy started to buck off the bed, causing Rip to pull his stiletto back out

"Knock it off, asshole." Rip held the blade up into Guy's crotch. "There are worse ways to leave this world."

With one hand on Guy's chest, pushing him back down into the bed, Mickey used his free hand to pull Guy's left arm into an outstretched position. Guy stopped fighting, but his muscles remained tense under Mickey's weight, causing the veins of his forearm to pop up under his skin.

Without any difficulty, Dr. Happy inserted the tip of the hypodermic needle into one of the engorged veins, puncturing through flesh until a flash of dark purple blood entered the syringe. Dr. Happy took his eyes off Guy's arm for a moment and glanced at his face. Guy was staring at him with a pleading expression, his eyes begging Dr. Happy for mercy. Dr. Happy's face offered no emotion in return. Without hesitation, he pushed the plunger of the syringe all the way in to the hilt.

Involuntarily, Guy made a deep, guttural, gasping noise that filled the hotel room. Rip and Mickey turned their eyes off Guy for a moment to silently acknowledge their shared sense of morbid fascination. Dr. Happy watched as Guy's pupils constricted to pinpoint size. Guy's body went limp and his breaths became shallower and shallower until they went away completely.

Rip caught Dr. Happy looking at his wristwatch. "What, are you calling the time of death, Doctor?"

"Sorry." Dr. Happy turned to face away from Rip. "Force of habit."

Rip sneered. "Those days are over, Marcus Welby." He grabbed Mickey. "All right, let's split." Turning back to Dr. Happy, he reached into the pocket of his sport coat and produced an envelope stuffed with cash. He tossed it onto the bed next to Guy's lifeless body. "That ought to cover parts and labor. Thanks as always for your service."

Dr. Happy kept silent as Rip and Mickey left the room, hoisting Bobby between them and carrying him out, one of his arms around a shoulder of each of them, like he was a drinking buddy who had one too many. Once the hotel door closed behind them, Dr. Happy checked his watch again. Two minutes had passed since Guy stopped breathing. He hurried to the side of the bed and checked Guy's wrist for a pulse, allowing only fifteen seconds for the task. He then reached back into his black medical bag and produced another prefilled syringe, this one with a piece of red tape wrapped around the cylinder. He attached a needle to the tip and reached for Guy's arm. The veins were less prominent now, so Dr. Happy blindly inserted the needle into the crease at Guy's elbow, twisting the syringe slightly in one direction and another, hoping to hit a vein by chance. He glanced at his watch. Three minutes, fifty seconds. He turned his attention back to the syringe. Pausing to take a deep breath, Dr. Happy withdrew the needle a fraction of an inch before changing the angle and reinserting it into Guy's arm. A blush of blood filled the syringe and Dr. Happy exhaled as he injected two milligrams of naloxone into Guy's bloodstream.

Almost immediately, Guy lurched up from the bed, gasping for air and sweating profusely. He looked up at Dr. Happy in confused panic.

"Wh-what did you do?" he stammered.

Dr. Happy's face was still devoid of expression. "*Primum non nocere,*" he answered.

# CHAPTER 12

"Where are we going?" Guy said. He was huddled up in a fetal position, shivering in the back seat of Dr. Happy's car. "Where are you taking me?"

Guy had stopped sweating and his salivary glands had calmed down to the point where he could open his mouth without drooling all over himself, but his head was still throbbing with pain. The entire left side of his face was swelling up, thanks to the working over that Rip and Mickey had provided, making it difficult for him to see out of that eye. The pain and decreased vision had made it difficult for Guy to discern the path they had followed after Dr. Happy, having revived him, grabbed Guy and led him out of the hotel room. Guy knew he was in a car, traveling very fast, but he couldn't tell which direction they were going in. Making matters worse, he couldn't get a read on Dr. Happy's intentions. Was he taking Guy to a hospital or to someplace where he could dispose of Guy more discreetly than in the hotel? Guy wondered: was he still in the frying pan, or had he fallen into the fire?

"Look, whatever game you're playing here," Guy sputtered over the top of the front seat, "this good cop, bad cop routine." Guy's words came out in gasping breaths. "You can spare yourself the effort. I don't know where she is."

Dr. Happy watched the road intently, his hands neatly

placed at ten and two o'clock on the steering wheel. "No," he said. "But you know where she's been."

Before Guy could react, Dr. Happy cut the steering wheel to the left, throwing Guy up against the right-side panel as the car took a sharp turn into a covered parking garage. Dr. Happy steered the car into a vacant spot in the corner of the garage farthest from the pedestrian elevator. Few cars occupied this section of the lot, and there was an eerie quiet once Dr. Happy put the car into park and killed the engine.

Dr. Happy turned so he was facing Guy, looking at him again with the same emotionless stare.

"Stay in the car," Dr. Happy instructed, breaking the silence. Guy complied, surprised to find Dr. Happy's delivery neither threatening nor demanding, but rather like he was simply offering very good advice.

In one fluid motion, Dr. Happy opened the driver's side door, stepped out of the car, closed the driver's side door, opened the rear passenger door, and slid into the back seat beside Guy. "Now move over," he told Guy once back inside the car.

Guy did as instructed. "Whatever you plan on doing to me," he said in hushed tone, "if the choice is another shot of smack or the other thing you gave me, at this point I might just choose the smack."

"Stop talking." Dr. Happy reached forward for Guy's face. Guy reflexively recoiled from him. "Don't move," Dr. Happy said with an annoyed sigh. "I'm not going to hurt you."

With his thumb and forefinger, Dr. Happy stretched open Guy's right eye, the one that wasn't swollen halfway shut, and inspected his pupil. Dr. Happy reached into his black leather medical bag and removed his penlight before clicking it on and shining it in Guy's eye. "Your pupils are normal in size and reacting to light appropriately."

"Is that good?" Guy asked.

Dr. Happy didn't respond but instead took Guy's wrist between his thumb and forefinger to check his pulse. After several seconds, Dr. Happy removed the blood pressure cuff from his bag and wrapped it around Guy's left bicep. Pulling his stethoscope to his ears, Dr. Happy placed its bell onto the crook of Guy's elbow and started squeezing the cuff's hand bulb.

"What are you doing now?" Guy asked. "What do you want?"

Dr. Happy glanced at him impatiently. "This works better if you don't speak."

After watching the needle on the pressure gauge bounce and fall, Dr. Happy deflated the blood pressure cuff and returned it to his bag.

"Your vitals are stable," he said. "I don't think you need another shot of Narcan."

"Okay." Guy assumed for the moment that was good news.

"In response to your earlier query, I am neither going to give you another shot of smack nor am I going to give you the other thing." Dr. Happy paused and shifted his weight so that the distance between the two became slightly greater and therefore less uncomfortable. "As to what I am doing now," he continued, "I am going to patch up your face so that, when you get out of this car, passersby are less likely to be so concerned with your appearance that they call the police. And finally, in regards to what I want," Dr. Happy dropped his medical bag onto the seat between them, "I want the same thing you do. I want to be free from Antonin Casparo."

Guy paused. "Easier said than done," Guy said. "How do you plan on achieving that?"

"By tracing your old girlfriend's steps," Dr. Happy answered. He reached into his medical bag and retrieved a tube of antibiotic ointment, a cotton-tipped applicator, and a pack of Steri-Strips. "If Casparo wants her as dead as Rip says, it's because she's got something big on him." After putting on a pair of fresh latex gloves, he squeezed a pea-sized amount of ointment onto the applicator and began smearing it over the cut above Guy's left eye. "We need to find out what that is."

Guy studied Dr. Happy as he applied the Steri-Strips to the cut, closing the wound. Dr. Happy's movements were precise and methodical, as if he were assembling a model airplane rather than providing medical care. His face still lacked any hint of sentiment, making it impossible for Guy to determine if he was lying or telling the truth. Guy considered his options. If the man applying butterfly stitches to his lacerated face was lying, then that meant he just wanted to find Blair so he could hand her over to Rip. In that case, Guy could go along with the story, and, as long as Guy didn't offer any information that this man didn't already have, then Guy wasn't putting Blair in any more danger than she was already in. And by playing along, Guy might gather some new information on Blair's whereabouts and would be able to skip out at the first possible opportunity. If the man next to him was lying and Guy instead refused, then without question Guy would find himself back in Rip's company with an exponentially shortened life expectancy, and Guy couldn't do anything to protect Blair if he were dead. On the other hand, if the man next to him was telling the truth, then that meant he was calling an audible and crossing Rip and Casparo, which gave them the common goal of finding Blair and keeping her in one piece. If that were the case, then even if this man proved untrustworthy, Guy could leverage his knowledge of that double-cross, if it came to that.

It also meant that this man had truly saved Guy's life. Which probably counted for something.

Guy rubbed at his jaw. "Okay, genius," he said. "If that's the play, then where do we start?"

"Her last known residence." Dr. Happy scanned Guy's face, inspecting his work before removing the latex gloves and tossing them onto the floor of the car. "The inpatient psychiatric unit on Beverly Boulevard."

Guy reached an exploratory finger up to the fresh bandages above his eye, keeping his gaze fixed on Dr. Happy. "We're just going to walk right in there?"

"We'll have to exercise a modicum of discretion," he answered. "But we will be walking in there."

Guy narrowed his eyes. "Are you really a doctor?" he asked.

"Do you really want to find Blair?" Dr. Happy replied.

"Yes."

"Then stop asking questions," Dr. Happy said. "If fact, try not to speak at all. When I need information from you, I'll ask for it. Until then, stay back here and try not to bleed anymore."

Guy felt his cheeks get hot. "Just so you know," he warned, "I've spent the better part of the last decade in the employ of the desperate and dishonorable. I can spot a scumbag when I see one. It doesn't matter what you call yourself or how smart you think you are. If you're not on the level, I'll know. And you may or may not live to regret it."

"Duly noted," Dr. Happy deadpanned. He opened the car door and returned to the driver's seat, leaving Guy alone in the back seat. He calmly inserted the key back in the ignition and as the engine turned over, he said to Guy: "But just so you know, I've seen and done things that your so-called desperate and dishonorable couldn't even begin to fathom. So you might reconsider putting me in the same category as the popcorn pimps that you're used to." He put the car into gear and added: "And if I weren't on the level, you'd still be without a pulse."

"Fair enough. My name's Guy McCann by the way." He coughed, trying to clear the blood and snot that had settled deep in his windpipe. "What do I call you?"

"You can call me Dr. Happy."

Guy frowned. "Is that your legal name?"

Dr. Happy responded by popping the clutch and gunning the engine, the sudden acceleration whipping Guy back against the leather upholstery as the car sped out of the garage.

# CHAPTER 13

Within the half hour they were back at the hospital. Dr. Happy got out of the car and motioned for Guy to follow him. Deciding for the moment to play along, Guy complied, trailing behind as they walked through a service entrance and down a hallway into the laundry facility. Once there, Dr. Happy inspected a row of freshly pressed white lab coats hanging from a large commercial clothing rack. He selected a forty-two long, pulled it off its hanger, and put it on.

"Do I get one too?" Guy asked.

Dr. Happy gestured toward Guy's face. "You won't be able to pull it off in your current condition," he said. "If anyone asks what you're doing, just tell them you got lost trying to find the ER."

Guy followed Dr. Happy as they walked back through the hallway to an elevator bay, where a courtesy telephone was affixed to the wall. Dr. Happy took the receiver from the cradle and it began ringing.

"Inpatient psych," Dr. Happy requested once the operator picked up and asked how she could assist him. After a few seconds, a female voice picked up.

"Twelfth floor."

"Hi, this is Dr. Montenegro," Dr. Happy said. "I was just paged to this number."

"Please hold."

Guy frowned. "What are you doing?" he asked.

Dr. Happy held up an index finger to his pursed lips.

"I'm sorry," the receptionist said, returning to the line. "It doesn't look like anyone paged you. What did you say your name was?"

"Dr. Montenegro. I just received a 911 page to this extension. Whoever's trying to reach me must need something urgently. It probably has to do with my patient, Blair Weston. She was admitted two nights ago for observation."

There was a pause on the line. "Um…" Another pause. "You mean no one's told you yet?"

"Told me what?" Dr. Happy said with feigned curiosity, transferring the receiver to his other ear.

"She eloped the night before last, Dr. Montenegro," the voice said. "She's not here anymore."

"Well, that is unfortunate, although not altogether surprising," Dr. Happy said. "She is very unstable and capable of just about anything." He took a deep breath close to the receiver so the receptionist could hear it over the phone. "Well, I'm going to need to come up and document all this in her chart. Could you please let the ward attending know I'm on my way?"

"Of course."

"Oh, who is on service right now?" Dr. Happy asked. "Is it whatshername?"

"No, Dr. Delgado is on vacation," the receptionist answered. "The attending is Dr. Casstevens."

"Thank you. Tell the doctor I'll be up in five minutes."

Dr. Happy hung up, then picked the phone back up and asked to be connected to the page operator.

"This is the parking garage," he said once the page operator picked up. "Can you please page Dr. Casstevens from psychiatry? We think his car has just been stolen. Thank you."

He hung up the phone and Guy followed him to one of the elevators.

"It's a locked unit, you know," Guy informed Dr. Happy. "The elevators won't go to the twelfth floor without a passkey or something."

"Oh, is that so?" Dr. Happy said. He then reached into his bag and retrieved a key ring, flipping through the keys until he found a large brass one with the word MASTER engraved on the bow. He threaded the blade into a keyhole that was next to the elevator button marked 12. After giving the key a quarter turn clockwise, he pressed the button and the elevator started rising.

Guy felt a pang of disappointment. "Where did you get that?"

"Don't worry about it."

"Whatever," Guy said. "When you finally decide to tell me what the hell you're doing, just give it all to me at once."

The elevator doors opened and they stepped out. Next to the elevator was a small cast iron bench, the floor around it littered with cigarette butts. Dr. Happy motioned to the bench. "You should wait here," he said. "I'll be right back."

Guy watched in silent frustration as Dr. Happy strolled down the hall that led to the psychiatric unit. He resigned himself to falling back into the bench and placing his head in his hands. The naloxone had long worn off, outlasted by some residual effects of the morphine injection. But now that too was fading and Guy became acutely aware that he was getting a hangover. That and his sense of increasing loss of control was making him rethink his strategy.

Meanwhile, Dr. Happy walked toward the psych unit, keeping his posture upright, reminding himself that if he could convince himself that he belonged there, he could convince others as well. As he approached the door to the psychiatric unit, a doctor burst through and rushed past him with a panicked look on his face. Dr. Happy suppressed a smile as he sidestepped the doctor and caught the closing unit door before the latch hit the strike plate. He slipped through and made sure the door closed behind him.

Dr. Happy confidently approached the receptionist's desk, situated behind a partition enclosed with plexiglass.

"I'm Dr. Montenegro," Dr. Happy said through the glass. "We spoke on the phone a minute ago."

"You just missed Dr. Casstevens," she said. "He had to step off the unit for a moment."

"Did he?" Dr. Happy replied. "That's okay. While I wait, may I please see my patient's chart?"

The receptionist opened the door to the partitioned nursing station and carefully closed it once Dr. Happy had entered. The receptionist motioned to a rack in the corner that housed several plastic notebooks, each with a patient's last name written on the spine in large capital letters. Dr. Happy took the chart marked "WESTON" and flipped through it. He checked the spine and read the room number underneath Blair's last name.

"I'll be right back," he told the receptionist as he walked back out of the nursing station and down the hallway of the psychiatric unit, toward room 133. He knocked gently on the door to announce his arrival. He opened the door and walked inside.

In the corner of the room, sitting on top of one of the two plastic mattresses bolted to the floor, was a nervous-looking woman in her forties wearing a pair of disposable scrubs. Dr. Happy smiled. "I heard your roommate ran away," he said.

The woman just nodded.

"Did she say where she was going?"

The woman offered no answer.

"Did she tell you anything at all?"

The woman's gaze fell to her feet. "She told me I needed to lose some weight."

"I see," Dr. Happy said, offering a consoling nod.

Dr. Happy spent five minutes poking around the room but

failed to find anything of interest. He then walked back to the nursing station.

"Did my patient leave any personal belongings?" Dr. Happy asked a tired-looking nurse once he was back behind the partition. "Do you still have the clothes she was wearing when she was admitted?"

The nurse reached behind a file folder, pulling back a brown paper bag, folded over and stapled shut. She pulled the bag open and pushed it over to Dr. Happy to inspect.

"Not much in there," she said. "Just a sweater, a pair of jeans, and her purse."

Dr. Happy opened the faux Louis Vuitton handbag and sifted through the contents. He noted a couple credit cards with expiration dates that had already passed. A few loose dollar bills and coins. Foundation and applicator. Nothing else.

"Just the kind of junk you find a purse," the nurse pointed out.

"She didn't have any meds on her?" Dr. Happy asked.

"Nope." The nurse shook her head. "Nothing personal either. You know, pictures or keepsakes. I noticed the driver's license is expired. There's nothing in there she even really needed."

"Nothing she couldn't replace," Dr. Happy said.

"Nope. The purse isn't even real leather. No wonder she didn't mind leaving it."

"Anything else that might help figure where she might have gone to?" Dr. Happy asked.

The nurse just shook her head. Dr. Happy was getting up to leave when she added: "Except for the arm thing I guess."

Dr. Happy stopped. "The arm thing?"

"Yeah."

"What arm thing?"

"No one told you?" the nurse said in amazement. She reached over, grabbed Blair's chart, and opened it. A mylar sleeve had been inserted inside the chart, and inside the sleeve were Polaroid pictures of a woman's right arm. "One of the other nurses saw the marks when she was changing into her hospital scrubs," the nurse explained. "She thought it was self-mutilation at first. You know, like she was a cutter. So the overnight resident took some pictures to document it."

Dr. Happy went through the pictures. On the inside of Blair's right arm, a seven-digit number had been written in permanent black ink.

"They asked what the numbers meant, but she wouldn't say," the nurse continued. "Acted like she didn't even know how they got there. But I bet she was just screwing with them."

"What makes you say that?"

She pointed to one of the pictures. "See how the first couple numbers are smudged? Like someone rubbed them when the ink was still wet?"

Dr. Happy nodded.

"That's what happens when someone who's left-handed writes with ink," the nurse explained. "Your hand smears the ink as you go from left to right. The numbers are written on her right arm. So, she probably wrote the numbers herself."

Dr. Happy was surprised to find himself somewhat impressed. She offered a modest grin. "I'm left-handed."

"That means that the right side of your brain is larger than most people's," Dr. Happy said. "Supposedly associated with superior intellect."

"Yeah, well." The nurse gestured toward the picture of Blair. "Clearly I'm in good company."

# CHAPTER 14

After a few minutes of sitting by himself on the bench, Guy got antsy and started pacing. He looked around for a clock to check the time but didn't find one. He then decided he needed to go to the bathroom but couldn't find one of those either. Irritated, he pressed the elevator down button and stepped into one of the cars once it arrived. Once inside, he remembered that he couldn't go anywhere without Dr. Happy's master key. Frustration boiled up within him and Guy smashed his fingers haphazardly into the different elevator buttons, jabbing them as hard as he could. This had no effect until he accidentally pushed the red emergency button. Immediately a ringing noise filled the elevator car. Guy pushed the red button again and the ringing stopped. He then noticed the emergency telephone attached to the elevator wall within a recessed compartment under the elevator buttons. He lifted the receiver and it began to ring.

"Maintenance," a raspy voice answered on the other line. "You have an emergency?"

"Um, sort of," Guy replied. "I got in the elevator and for some reason it took me straight up to the twelfth floor. Now I can't get back down."

"What the hell?" the voice answered. "All right, just hold tight. We're going to call the car back down the first floor."

Guy hung up the phone and leaned back against the wall of

the elevator. After several minutes, the car descended and when the doors opened, Guy found himself in the hospital lobby. Outside the elevator car were a maintenance worker and a skinny security guard, both of whom were eyeing him suspiciously.

"Where were you trying to go?" the guard asked.

Guy pointed to his left eye. "Got lost trying to find the ER."

The guard's gaping jaw acknowledged Guy's swollen face. "Jeez, you don't say, Mister. It's down the hall. Follow signs for Emergency."

Guy thanked him and started walking. Once out of sight from the elevator bay, he hung a left and ducked into a men's room. Inside, he stood in front of one of the sinks and inspected his reflection in the mirror. His left eyelid had almost entirely swollen shut, but the cartilage in his nose was in one piece and none of his teeth had been knocked loose. The Steri-Strips were still in place, keeping the ends of the cut well approximated. He turned on the faucet and held his head under the spigot. He swished the warm, stale-tasting tap water around in his mouth and spit it out into the sink, sending several blood clots with it. He turned off the faucet and watched the mixture of blood and water swirl down the drain before walking out.

Guy scanned the lobby, looking for anyone who might be employed by Casparo in case Rip had thought to come to the hospital to look for clues for Blair, like he and Dr. Happy had. The current occupants of the lobby seemed harmless enough, mostly patients in faded hospital-issue pajamas tethered to IV poles, their jaundiced skin betraying their rapidly approaching expiration dates. Guy pretended they weren't there, uninterested in how their presence reminded him that his days too were likely numbered. He found the coffee stand near the entrance of the hospital lobby and shuffled over to it.

The coffee stand proprietor shot Guy a curious look when he approached.

"What happened to your face?"

Guy shrugged. "Punched myself shaving."

The barista wrinkled his face. "What?"

"Never mind," Guy said. "Can I get a cup of black coffee?"

"Ho'kay."

Guy fished around in his front pocket and produced two quarters, which he dropped on the counter. The barista returned with the coffee. Guy took a sip and the hot liquid shot a spasm of pain into his swollen upper lip.

"You wouldn't have any ice, would you?" he asked.

"For your face?"

"Yeah."

The barista shook his head. "You know you're in a hospital, right? Why don't you see a doctor?"

"I did," Guy answered, pointing to the butterfly stitches above his eye.

"He wouldn't give you any ice?"

Guy shook his head.

"That's not a nice doctor," the barista said.

"Understatement of the century," Guy muttered.

Guy took his coffee and sat down at one of the small tables off the side of the lobby and wrapped both hands around the Styrofoam cup. He hardly noticed when Dr. Happy walked up to him.

"I overheard there was a man with a black eye wandering around the hospital looking suspicious," Dr. Happy said. "After your girlfriend's Houdini act, they're probably real sensitive to that sort of thing around here." He took a seat across from Guy. "So I wouldn't bother trying to give me the slip again, at least not here. You might find it harder than you'd think."

Guy shook his head. "I wasn't skipping out," he said. "My head won't stop pounding." Guy motioned to the cup of coffee in his hand. "I needed something for the pain. You ever experience a concussion and a hangover at the same time?"

"It'll pass," Dr. Happy replied. "I examined your face. Nothing's broken. There's nothing to do until the swelling goes down except maybe take some ibuprofen."

"You holding?" Guy asked.

Dr. Happy shook his head. "Nothing that soft, no."

Guy frowned and took another sip from his coffee cup.

Dr. Happy drummed his fingertips on the tabletop for several seconds before taking a deep breath and leaning in across the table so he was closer to Guy. "I need to ask you something. Is Blair left-handed?"

Guy thought it over. "How would I know?" he replied. "I don't think I ever saw her write anything."

Dr. Happy lowered his voice. "Did she ever give you an old fashioned?"

Guy wrinkled his forehead and shot Dr. Happy a sideways glance. "You know," he began, leaning back in his chair to increase the distance between the two of them, "you and I just met."

"Which hand did she use?"

Guy paused for a moment. "Yeah," he answered. "She's left-handed."

Dr. Happy produced the picture from Blair's chart, sliding it across the table to Guy and pointing to the numbers written on her arm. "See that? I think Blair wrote those numbers on her arm."

Guy shifted in his seat. "Why would she do that?" he asked, taking the Polaroid so that he could inspect it closer.

"Everything Blair's done so far that I know about," Dr. Happy began, "I have no idea why anyone would do them. Do the numbers mean anything to you?"

Guy shook his head.

"It's seven digits long," Dr. Happy said. "Could it be a phone number? A safe combination, map coordinates, anything?"

"Map coordinates?" Guy was growing annoyed. "You saw her picture. Does she look like Horatio Hornblower to you? I told you, I don't know what the numbers mean. None of this makes any sense." He threw the picture down on the table and crossed his arms over his chest.

"If you were as close to Blair as you've let on, then you know her better than most," Dr. Happy began. "Walk me through what you know about her recent activity."

Guy's gut still told him to hold his cards close, not give away anything that might put Blair in further jeopardy. "You know everything I do," Guy said. "You saw her hotel room, the Polaroids she took. If you saw her chart, then you know why they stuck her in the psych ward."

"But why?" Dr. Happy asked. "Why the pictures in the ballpark?"

"I don't know." Guy stood up quickly, almost knocking over his chair behind him as he rose. "Maybe she really does need psychiatric attention. Maybe living that life broke her down and now she's just trying to stay alive."

"If it were that, then why did she leave the psych ward?" Dr. Happy rose from his own chair and stepped toward Guy. "It's a locked unit with around-the-clock security. She would have been safe there. What other reason would she have to get herself committed? What could she have possibly stood to gain from spending one night in the hospital?"

"I don't know!" Guy stepped backward to put more space between him and Dr. Happy. As he did this, he bumped into the person behind him, a gaunt geriatric in a faded hospital gown. The man glared at Guy with a pair of deep-set, hollow eyes.

"Sorry," Guy absently apologized without turning around. He was still looking at Dr. Happy with an intense glare. "What if she just was trying…"

He was interrupted by the man in the hospital gown, who had walked up to Guy, lifted a slipper-clad foot, and stepped on Guy's shoe with obvious intent.

Guy turned toward the old man and shot him a confused look. "Did you just step on my foot?"

The man wore a sardonic smile. "Now *I'm* sorry," he said through yellow, gritted teeth. "How does that feel?"

"Are you serious?" Guy asked. "Are you really starting something with me?"

"Don't start thinking." The patient shook his head side to side in a condescending manner. "Don't start thinking."

Guy was still having trouble processing what was happening. He noticed the man in the hospital gown was pulling alongside him an IV pole, from which hung a large plastic bag full of a neon yellow liquid that dripped through a length of plastic tubing to a catheter inserted in his right arm. "Thinking about what?" Guy asked. "Your decreasing life expectancy?"

A flash of color filled the patient's otherwise ashen countenance and he stuck a boney finger in Guy's face. "Don't start thinking," he kept muttering.

"It's too late, Karen Carpenter." Guy took a step closer to the patient. "I'm already thinking. Thinking about teaching you what it really means to be sorry."

Before Guy could take another step, a hospital security guard placed an arm across his chest and pushed him backward.

"Are you actually getting into a fight with this patient?" The guard seemed more disgusted with Guy than angry.

Guy stood silently, a wave of shame washing over him.

"He has cancer, man," the guard exclaimed with a pointed tone. "You've already won."

The show over, the small crowd that had gathered in the lobby started to disperse. The cancer patient grabbed his IV pole and wheeled it down the hall, shaking his head and continuing to mutter to himself.

"You're unusually quiet," Guy said to Dr. Happy. "What? No color commentary?"

"That patient's wrist," he answered.

Guy shot a glance down the hall the cancer patient had retreated to. "What about it?"

"He was wearing a hospital bracelet," Dr. Happy continued. "It had his medical record number printed on it."

"So?"

"So," Dr. Happy said, "it's seven digits long."

Guy was getting pretty sick of being led around the hospital, like a little kid on Halloween who'd rather be at home watching TV but whose parents insist on forcing him to go door-to-door trick-or-treating in an ill-fitting homemade costume. But he also couldn't deny the fluttering in his chest triggered by the thought that they might be a step closer to finding Blair.

"You're sure that the number on Blair's arm is a medical record number?" he asked as he followed down a first-floor hallway, one pace behind Dr. Happy.

Dr. Happy shook his head. "Not positive. But it's worth looking into, and easy enough to check out." He was leading Guy toward a sign that read *Medical Records.*

"Why would she write it on her arm?" Guy asked. "In permanent marker?"

"Think about it," Dr. Happy answered. "When you get admitted to a psychiatric unit, they take away your clothes and all your personal belongings. If Blair needed to keep something on her, if she needed that number for something important, her only option was to secure it to her person."

"But still, if faking psychosis to get into this hospital was part of some sort of grand master plan of hers, you'd think she'd be able to memorize a seven-digit number. It's no longer than a phone number."

"They admitted her involuntarily," Dr. Happy countered. "They could have chemically restrained her as well."

"You mean drugged her?"

"Medicated," Dr. Happy corrected. "Five milligrams of Haldol and two milligrams of Ativan would have caused quite a memory retrieval deficit. Writing it on her arm may have been an insurance policy."

They reached the Medical Records office and walked inside. There was a small anteroom separated from a large library by a counter with a sliding glass partition for security purposes. Behind the partition sat a slack-jawed kid in his twenties who Guy surmised had gotten the job as part of a state-sponsored work placement program for reformed paint huffers. Behind him were rows and rows of file cabinets filled with medical charts, all labeled with seven-digit numbers.

"Excuse me," Dr. Happy said, leaning over the counter. "I need to review a patient's records. It's for an M&M and they only gave me the MRN. Are you able to pull the chart with just that?"

"Sure," the kid behind the counter replied. "What's the number?"

Dr. Happy recited the seven digits that Blair had written on her arm, which the kid scribbled down onto a piece of scrap paper.

"Be right back," the kid informed him.

Dr. Happy turned back to Guy. "You know," he said. "It isn't the easiest thing to break out of a psychiatric unit."

Guy shrugged. "She bribed that security guard Frank."

"She didn't have anything on her except a pair of hospital scrubs," Dr. Happy said. "What did she bribe him with?"

Guy raised an eyebrow. It was enough for Dr. Happy to catch his drift.

"Classy broad," Dr. Happy replied.

"It worked," Guy countered.

The kid returned to the counter with a guilty look on his face. "Um," he stumbled. "I'm really sorry but that chart is missing."

Dr. Happy frowned. "Could it be somewhere else?"

The kid shook his head. "If it were being processed by medical-legal it would say so in the computer."

"Maybe someone left it on one of the units," Dr. Happy suggested.

"I checked," the kid replied. "But it hasn't been signed out in weeks. It's just...missing."

"Or stolen?" Guy countered.

The kid was taken aback by the suggestion. "I'd hate to think that's the case. Anyway, how would someone be able to steal it?"

Guy considered the question. "What time does this office close?"

"Five p.m.," the kid answered. He then noticed Guy's swollen left eye for the first time. "Whoa, what happened to your face?"

"Shut up," Guy replied. "So after five, someone could break in and there wouldn't be anyone here to see them?"

"Yeah," the kid mumbled. "But with the hospital security the way it is, to gain access back here, it would have to be a hospital employee."

Guy's mind went back to the cancer patient with the IV pole, roaming the halls of the hospital without anyone batting an eyelash. "What about a patient?" he asked.

"Huh?" The kid scratched at his nose.

"An admitted patient wouldn't need to worry about getting past security to get into the hospital," Guy said. "What would keep someone who was already in the hospital from being able to get into the records room after hours?"

The kid wrinkled his brow. "This glass window, I guess."

Guy turned his attention to the sliding glass partition that separated him and Dr. Happy from the kid. At that moment it was fully open. Guy reached over and pulled it closed. Along the edge of the partition was a flimsy brass lock that could be pried open with little more than a hairpin.

The kid shrugged. "I guess that *could* happen," he said, but his voice lacked conviction. "But it's probably just in transit somewhere. I'm sure it'll turn up."

"Sure," Dr. Happy said. "Thanks for your time."

"Check back tomorrow," the kid said. "If Mr. Casparo's chart shows up, I'll have it held here at the desk for you."

"Thanks," Dr. Happy said. He turned to leave the counter but then stopped suddenly. Guy felt the blood rush away from his face.

"Wait, what?" Dr. Happy asked, his voice taking an impatient tone.

The kid seemed confused by Dr. Happy's reaction. "I said I'll have the chart held here for you if it turns up."

"*Whose* chart?"

"Oh, that's right," the kid said. "I forgot you didn't know the patient's name. I wrote it down for you." He glanced down at the scrap of paper in his hand. "It's Casparo. Antonin Casparo."

# CHAPTER 15

"Is there anything in your motel room that you can't live without?" Dr. Happy asked. They were back in Dr. Happy's car, this time with Guy riding shotgun, heading east on Santa Monica Boulevard toward Hollywood.

Guy shook his head. Aside from the clothes he had worn on his drive to LA, the only thing he had left in the motel room was what was left in the bottle of Dewar's. Which technically he could live without.

"Because I'm sure you've surmised by now that we can't go back there."

"And I'm guessing you're also persona non grata by now."

Dr. Happy unclipped his beeper from his belt and held it up in front of him, his gaze alternating between its display and the road ahead of him. "I started getting pages two hours after we left Blair's hotel room. That's when Rip figured something was wrong. The pages stopped about an hour ago. That's when Rip figured I flipped."

"So you think Rip's been on our tail for about an hour?"

Dr. Happy nodded.

"How long did it take him to find me?" Guy asked.

"Less than twenty-four hours," Dr. Happy replied.

"Shit," Guy muttered. "I thought this was a big town."

"Men like Rip, they know enough to make it a small town."

Guy rubbed his chin in consideration. "So, how much time do you think we have to find Blair before Rip finds us?"

Dr. Happy slowed the car and pulled into the parking lot of a nondescript motel off Melrose Avenue. "Just depends on which problem is the bigger priority for him. Us or Blair."

"I have a feeling that thanks to you the three of us are all just one big problem for Rip right now," Guy replied.

"Before that train of thought gets too far from the station," Dr. Happy began, "don't forget it's thanks to me you're feeling anything right now."

The two exited the car without any further conversation. At the entrance of the motel there was a small office with battered venetian blinds shielding the glass door from the outside world. Guy and Dr. Happy entered in silence and found a pudgy, pockmarked clerk behind a counter. As the two walked inside, he peered at them behind thick-rimmed eyeglasses.

"Room for the night?" he asked, discarding the magazine he had been occupying himself with.

"Two rooms," Guy clarified.

"You sure?" The clerk raised both eyebrows. "If you two want just one room, it's cool."

"I'm sure it is," Guy said. "But I imagine it would be even cooler if we paid for two rooms."

"Twenty each for the night then. Two-dollar towel deposit."

Guy reached into his pocket, realizing that he had given his last ten dollars to the pimp the night before. He started thinking of a way to ask Dr. Happy to spring for his room, without the clerk double-checking that they didn't really want just a single, before he stumbled on something in his right hip pocket. He withdrew his right hand and pulled out a black leather wallet. His eyes brightened. He opened the wallet and pulled a credit card out of one of seamed pouches.

"Do you take American Express?" he asked.

The clerk took the card from Guy and ran it through the imprinter, then handed the duplicate slip and the credit card to

Guy along with a ballpoint pen. Guy quickly scrawled an illegible signature on the charge slip, trying to keep a straight face. The clerk took the slip and tore free the duplicate sheet and slid it and two room keys across the counter toward Guy.

"1213 and 1215," the clerk said. "Enjoy your stay, Mr. Mancuso."

Guy pocketed the card and slip, gripping the room keys tightly with his other hand, and started down the walkway toward the motel patio. Dr. Happy caught up to him.

"Mr. Mancuso?" he inquired.

Guy handed Dr. Happy the wallet. Dr. Happy flipped it open to the driver's license inside.

"This is Rip's," Dr. Happy quickly deduced.

"Rip and his goons might turn the town upside down looking for me, but I doubt they're looking for rooms checked in under his name."

Dr. Happy considered this. "How did you get this?" he asked, holding out the wallet like it was medical waste.

"When Rip delivered that gut punch, it folded me in half." Guy took back the wallet without concern. "I practically fell into his lap. While I was trying to right myself, I felt his wallet in his jacket pocket. He was so geared up giving me the thrashing that he didn't even notice I palmed it."

"Why did you take it? You couldn't have assumed you were leaving that hotel room alive."

"So that when the cops found my corpse they'd have a clue who was responsible."

Dr. Happy slid his tongue along the inside of his cheek. "That is awful stubborn of you."

Guy didn't say anything in response.

The two reached their rooms and Guy unlocked the first door. Dr. Happy reached out for the second room key. "You probably want to get a couple hours of rest," he said. "But keep in mind, the longer we let Blair roam, the lower the chances of us finding her."

"Let me just show you some of her stuff that I found first. Maybe give you some ideas where we can go from here."

They walked into the motel room, barely noticing its drab, worn-down décor. Guy went straight to the bathroom and inspected his reflection in the vanity mirror. The swelling above his eye had not gotten any worse since the hospital. He took a hand towel from next to the sink and soaked it in cold water before wringing it dry and holding it up to his brow. When he left the bathroom, Dr. Happy was sitting at the edge of the bed, dragging his thumbnail across his chin.

"She left her purse behind on purpose," Dr. Happy said. "She knew she would have trouble getting it back, so she made sure there was nothing of value in it."

"Well, nothing of monetary value." Guy sat down in a chair in the corner. "But that's where I found her hotel key when I tried to find her in the ER. I took that out of her purse before the orderlies brought it up to the psych unit."

"So you think she was leaving bread crumbs for you?"

"I don't know," Guy said. "But I found more of Blair's stuff in her hotel room, and unlike the crap in her purse, I don't think she ditched any of it on purpose. Maybe she got wise that Rip had tracked her to the hotel, so she had no choice but to leave it behind."

"Could be why she picked that day to check herself into the psych unit," Dr. Happy mused. "So what did you find in the hotel room?"

Guy stood up and reached into his pockets. He tossed some of the Polaroid pictures over to Dr. Happy, who picked them up and flipped through them. He paused on the one of Blair inside the baseball stadium.

"You showed me this one already." He fanned the picture in the air absently. "And I saw another like it back in the hotel room. At the time I just thought she was crazy."

"So did the psych resident in the ER," Guy replied.

"Crazy enough to earn her a night in the hospital," Dr.

Happy said. "And now we know what that got her: Casparo's medical chart."

"But what's the play there?" Guy asked. "What does that score her?"

"Something Casparo doesn't want anyone other than his doctor to know," Dr. Happy answered. "Probably a blackmail angle. Is she capable of that?"

Guy considered the question. "I don't know. Her sister made it sound like she's in one of her states. When she gets like that…" He fell back into the chair. "I don't know."

Dr. Happy rested his hands in his lap, waiting a beat before he continued. "Maybe it would help if I knew more about Blair. What's her story, exactly?"

"She works for Anneleise Casparo."

"How'd she wind up doing that?"

"I don't know."

"You never asked?"

"We didn't spend our time together talking about stuff like that," Guy said. "How do most girls end up that way?"

"Usually by running up a drug debt," Dr. Happy answered, almost like he was surprised he had to explain it. "Then Anneleise gets them on the hook to pay it off, only she keeps the vig running so the girl never has the chance to pay her off."

Guy exhaled slowly. "Blair's not the after-school special type."

"I'm starting to wonder if you really know what type she is."

Guy's first instinct was to tell Dr. Happy to go fuck himself, but he hesitated for a split-second, and in that time realized that there were a lot of questions he never asked Blair. And if he was going to find her, Guy might need to learn some things about Blair that he didn't want to know. He scratched at the back of his head and dabbed the towel at his eye. He then reached back into his pocket and removed the prescription bottles he had taken from Blair's room. He tossed them over to Dr. Happy on the bed. "I found these in the room too. Can you tell me what the pills are for?"

Dr. Happy held up one of the bottles and inspected the label. "This is lithium," he answered. "This is for manic depression."

Guy watched as Dr. Happy twisted open a second bottle and tipped it over. Out of the bottle and into his open palm fell a plastic baggie filled with white powder. "And this is for something else," he said.

Guy's mouth fell open. "Is that what I think it is?"

Dr. Happy didn't answer. He just delicately placed the baggie onto the bed, some distance away from him.

Guy's eyes followed the baggie and caught the third of the prescription bottles lying next to it on the bed. He reached over and picket it up, squinting at the label. "Dexedrine?" he asked, as if making sure he was pronouncing it correctly.

"Let me see that."

Guy handed the bottle to Dr. Happy.

"These are amphetamines." Dr. Happy turned the bottle, reading further down on the label. "These weren't written to Blair though," he said. "They're for someone named Cam Del Rio." His gaze lifted from the bottle up to Guy. "Why does that name sound familiar?"

Guy shook his head. He then motioned to the stack of Polaroid pictures. "Of all the photos Blair took inside the ballpark, there were only a couple of players she shot. One guy was in practically all of them."

Dr. Happy spread out the pictures on the bed. Guy stood up and leaned over to look at them. He pointed to one of them.

"Him," Guy said, indicating a picture of a tall, dark-haired ballplayer on his way to home plate from the batter's circle. When Guy had first noticed how many pictures of this ballplayer Blair had taken, he had assumed she had just taken a liking to his physique. His biceps were so big that he could snap the baseball bat in half. "There were at least ten photos of him in Blair's hotel room."

"To be honest I don't follow the game much," Dr. Happy said.

"I didn't recognize him either," Guy admitted. "Must be only a couple of years in the pros. I haven't been able to keep up much in the desert."

"The desert?" Dr. Happy asked. "You mean Vegas? Is that where you've been hiding out from Casparo?"

Guy gritted his teeth, cursing himself for letting his guard down. Dr. Happy glanced back at him, seeming to sense the distrust in his expression. Dr. Happy's next words came out slowly and carefully.

"If I was out to get you," he began, "I'd have had plenty of opportunities to do so by now. And you've had plenty of chances to split if you wanted to. But neither of those things have happened yet. So do you think that maybe we can start trusting each other?"

"Maybe," Guy considered.

Dr. Happy picked up the picture off the bed. "Well, Blair apparently considers him a person of interest," he said. "So, how about we start by finding him and determine if he indeed is Cam Del Rio?"

Guy picked at his teeth with his thumbnail for several seconds before answering. "There's a card shop down the road," he finally replied. "I saw it on the drive in. We can check the current roster and see if it's him."

They headed out of the motel room.


To their relief, there was little activity near the entrance of the motel. Guy and Dr. Happy walked in silence two blocks down the street to the card shop that Guy had spotted as they had driven up to the motel earlier. A bell above the door rang as they entered. The shop was dank and cluttered. They were alone other than the overweight shopkeeper, who remained motionless as they walked into the store. Guy got the impression that he hadn't moved from his seat behind the register all day.

"Help you gentlemen?" the shopkeeper asked. His eyes

remained fixed on the newspaper spread out on the counter in front of him.

Guy approached the counter. "You have a home team set for this year?" he asked. "The whole team?"

The shopkeeper shifted his weight to help him maneuver off his stool. "I assume you mean Dem Bums?" he grunted. "Not those fairies in Orange County?"

"Um, yeah," Guy replied

The shopkeeper reached over and produced a three-ring binder from the display case that sat next to him. He rested the binder on the counter and opened it. Inside were several polypropylene sleeves, each displaying baseball trading cards, sixteen at a time in a four-by-four grid.

"This is the '86 Topps set," the shopkeeper grunted. "The '87 set comes out in January."

Guy flipped through the pages as Dr. Happy peered over his shoulder. Guy recognized a few of the players, the future hall-of-famers that had been on the roster for years, but most he wouldn't have noticed if he ran into them on the street.

"You looking to buy the set, or are you looking for a player in particular?" The shopkeeper sounded mildly annoyed by Guy's browsing.

Guy ignored him and continued through the binder. On one of the last sheets in the set he finally found Cam Del Rio. He thrust his forefinger onto the plastic sleeve protecting Del Rio's baseball card. "Found him."

Guy produced Blair's photograph. While the player in the Polaroid had considerably more muscle on his frame, his facial features confirmed that it was a match.

"Well, we confirmed that your girlfriend has a crush on Cam Del Rio," Dr. Happy said. His eyes scanned back and forth between the image in the Polaroid and that on the baseball card. "Jesus, he was skinny then."

"Who, Del Rio?" the shopkeeper chimed in. "He was just a rookie last year. They're all skin and bones when they first get called up. The minors are a bitch. They barely feed the kids in triple-A ball."

Guy offered a blank stare.

"I ought to know," the shopkeeper said, hitching at his belt. "I used to play."

"Of course you did." Guy noted the considerable circumference of the man's waistline.

The shopkeeper frowned. "Pitched for the Kansas City farm team. Almost got to the big club a couple times. I was famous for my knuckler."

"I'll have to take your word for it," Guy said. "I'm more of a football fan."

"Rams or Raiders?"

"Niners."

"Tourist," the shopkeeper muttered with disdain.

"Fuck you."

The shopkeeper shook his head. "Doesn't matter much anyway this year. The whole goddamn season's blown thanks to the strike. I'm not rooting for a bunch of scab football players. Now baseball, that's where the real athletes are. There's a reason it's still called America's favorite pastime."

Guy had stopped listening. He motioned to Dr. Happy. "All right," he said. "So now we need to find Cam Del Rio."

"Where do you suggest we start?"

Guy addressed the shopkeeper. "Is there a home game tonight?"

The shopkeeper nodded in response. "Playing the Giants," he said, then narrowed his eyes at Guy. "Your kind of game."

Guy let the last comment drift and turned back to Dr. Happy. "How far do you think we are from the stadium?"

"In traffic?" Dr. Happy asked. "Maybe half an hour at most."

Guy checked his watch. "That would give us plenty of time to find him in the clubhouse before the game starts. Think you can talk your way into the stadium?"

"Worth a short," Dr. Happy answered. "Worst-case scenario

they throw us out."

"I can live with that," Guy replied.

"We should ditch my car though," Dr. Happy said. "Rip knows what I drive."

"Then we need new wheels if we're going to get to the stadium."

"There's a car rental place nearby."

Guy considered. "The one on Wilshire and Burlington? Kind of high end."

"You still have Rip's credit card?"

Guy smiled. He then turned back to the shopkeeper. "Thanks for your help," he said, closing the binder. "But I think we're all done here."

"Hey," the shopkeeper objected. "You're not going to buy anything? What am I wasting my time showing you this stuff for? Bad enough I'm talking to a couple of sissies. But cheapskate sissies! That takes it."

"Jesus, calm down," Guy said. "What's your problem?"

"You two. You're my problem. This isn't a library."

Guy felt his neck get hot. "It isn't much of card shop either," he remarked. "There's no one in here in the middle of the afternoon and there's hardly any merch except what you have in the display glass. If I didn't think you were too stupid to pull it off, I'd swear this place was a front."

The shopkeeper's jaw dropped. "A what?" he stammered.

"A front," Guy repeated. "An illusory operation meant to conceal illegitimate criminal activity."

The shopkeeper frowned. "Get out of here," he said. "This ain't no front."

"Come on," Dr. Happy said to Guy. "Let's go."

"Hold on," Guy said. He turned back to the shopkeeper. "Isn't it? Exactly what are you running out of the back of this place? Grass? Poppers? Bootleg Chinese-made Transformers knockoffs?"

The shopkeeper's glasses steamed over.

"You know they use lead paint for those, right?" Guy asked. "It turns kids retarded." He appealed to Dr. Happy. "Help me out here."

"He is technically correct about the lead paint," Dr. Happy informed the shopkeeper. But his words had a reluctant delivery and he kept his gaze at the exit. "It can cause brain damage in children."

"What are you guys, cops?" the shopkeeper said. He was waving at them with his palms outstretched. "I run an honest store here, I swear."

"Says you," Guy shot back. "Next paycheck says he's got a cage full of Vietnamese potbellied pigs in the back room."

The shopkeeper's demeanor turned and his face went beet red as he shouted at Guy: "You get the hell out of here. Get out of my shop this minute."

Guy felt Dr. Happy's hand on his shoulder. "All right," Guy said. "Let's go."

The two turned to exit, leaving the fuming shopkeeper behind as he continued to shout at them. On their way out the door, Guy turned back and shot a sarcastic grin. "See you in the postseason, Knuckles," he said, before letting the door slam shut behind him.

"Was that absolutely necessary?" Dr. Happy asked once they were both outside. "If we're going to go through with this, then I need you to keep a little cooler than that."

"He pissed me off." Guy was pacing around the sidewalk, trying to burn off his anger. "I'm not letting an uneducated troglodyte like him talk to me like that."

"When we get to the stadium you better let me do the talking," Dr. Happy said. "If you pull anything like that there, you're going to get us arrested."

"Don't worry about me." Guy threw him a dirty look. "You're not the only professional here. But why couldn't you back me up a little better in there?" Guy's voice changed pitch. "I thought we were a team."

"We have a common goal," Dr. Happy said, "which is to

find Blair and find out what she has on Casparo. I fail to see how berating middle-aged small business owners is a required step in the pursuit of that goal."

"Well, it made me feel better."

"Did it?"

Guy lowered his head as they continued down the street. "No, not really."

# CHAPTER 16

Within the hour, Guy and Dr. Happy were in a car rental office two blocks away, being handed the keys to a Jaguar XJS convertible. There was an awkward moment when both Guy and Dr. Happy reached for the driver's door handle upon being escorted to the car in the lot. Still sore from the scene at the card shop, Guy readied a less than polite assertion for the right to drive the Jaguar. However, it turned out to be unnecessary as Dr. Happy stepped back and allowed Guy to proceed without any argument.

Once on the road, Guy lowered the cloth top and felt the breeze pass through him. He couldn't help but relax a notch, driving the convertible luxury car north on Highway 110. The late-afternoon traffic held them to low speeds, and the car exhaust on the gridlocked highway made the experience of driving with the top down less pleasant. But Guy, settled into the leather interior with his hands resting on the walnut steering wheel, found his mood improving nevertheless. His earlier frustration couldn't compete with the grace, space, and pace of the Jaguar.

After several minutes of stop and go on the 110, Guy turned to Dr. Happy to break the silence. "You didn't answer my question earlier."

"Which one?" Dr. Happy kept his eyes pointed forward.

"Are you really a doctor?"

"Does it matter?"

Guy thought about it. "I'm just curious. Most doctors I've met, particularly the ones I've met lately, have been pretty inept. But you seem to know what you're doing. I find it kind of ironic."

If Dr. Happy took this as a compliment, he kept it to himself.

Guy turned his attention back to the road and absently drummed his fingertips on the steering wheel. He turned back to Dr. Happy. "I'm really a lawyer, by the way."

Dr. Happy shook his head. "Yeah, I didn't ask," he said.

Guy exhaled slowly out his mouth. *Fuck that asshole*, Guy told himself. *Just enjoy the experience of this fine automobile.* His thoughts were interrupted by another driver cutting him off in traffic. Guy slammed on the brake and blared the horn while Dr. Happy silently fastened his seatbelt, a dour expression on his face.

It was a long ride to the stadium.


After Guy turned into the stadium parking lot, Dr. Happy directed him to the players' entrance. Guy parked the Jaguar and they both exited the car and walked toward the ballpark. Guy noted how Dr. Happy's conduct changed as they approached the gate. His posture improved and he was walking with his chin held high. He carried the confident air of someone who was supposed to be there, someone who viewed walking into a major league ballpark to talk to professional baseball players as an almost mundane task. This confidence was not lost on the guard standing outside the gate.

"Can I help you, sir?" he eagerly asked Dr. Happy.

"That would be very helpful," Dr. Happy began. "We're from the CDC. I need to talk to one of the team physicians."

"CDC?" the guard asked. "Don't you mean you need to talk to ownership?"

"No, it's just a routine investigation," Dr. Happy replied. "I wish I could go into more detail, but it's a bit of a sensitive matter."

"Does this have something to do with one of the players?" the guard asked.

"I may have said too much already."

The guard smiled. "Don't worry about it, doc. I don't see any visitors scheduled today, but they miss stuff all the time. If this is a medical matter, I suppose we should let you go on your business."

"I appreciate your assistance."

"All guests do have to check in with the security office and get a pass to enter the clubhouse, though," the guard informed them. "Follow me."

Guy got nervous at the mention of checking in with security, but he followed Dr. Happy's lead, who didn't seem to mind the idea at all. The two simply showed their drivers' licenses—Guy remembered to produce his own instead of Rip's—and they were issued temporary day passes that they displayed around their necks like Olympic medals. Another guard escorted the two to the clubhouse, he and Dr. Happy trading snide comments about the team's sub-.500 record while Guy tried to suppress his excitement. The last time he had been in a baseball stadium he was just a kid. He had to ignore the dizzyingly magical atmosphere—a place where dreams came to be either accomplished or trampled on—lest he tip his hand in front of the security detail.

The guard led them through a blue fire door and into the players' locker room. As soon as they arrived, an older man in a blue windbreaker with the team logo on the back approached them.

"I'm Marcus Polley, one of the assistant physicians," he said, looking at Guy and Dr. Happy curiously. "This is the first I've heard about any CDC investigation. May I ask what this is about?"

"Of course," Dr. Happy replied. He produced one of the photographs of Blair. "Have you seen this woman fraternizing with any of the players?"

Dr. Polley squinted at the picture, then looked back at Dr. Happy. "What if I did?"

"As you know, syphilis is a reportable disease." Dr. Happy took on an exasperated attitude. "We at the CDC have the responsibility of tracking the spread of its infection in order to prevent a potential epidemic."

Guy involuntarily shot Dr. Happy a stunned look at the mention of the word *syphilis*.

Dr. Polley followed Dr. Happy's explanation, apparently not noticing Guy breaking character. "Shit," he whispered. "Is that what this is about?"

"I'm afraid so," Dr. Happy answered. "And we have reason to believe that our index patient may have exposed some of your players."

"Some of them?" Polley asked. "You mean she's been with more than one?"

"Apparently that's how they're doing it these days."

Polley shook his head with a look of disapproval. "Jesus," he muttered under his breath.

"You can be assured that CDC investigations this sensitive in nature are performed under the strictest discretion."

"Oh, I trust you two to keep this discreet." Polley waved a hand as he dismissed Dr. Happy's implication. "I'm just a little disappointed in the boys is all."

"Of course," Dr. Happy said in response. "I'd feel the same way if it happened to one of my patients." He looked around the locker room. "However, we are going to need to speak to some of your players and take some blood samples to run VDRL and RPR assays. Rest assured if any of the boys test positive, we'll provide the penicillin treatment free of cost."

"I'm not worried about that," Polley replied. "Which boys do you two need to see?"

Dr. Happy produced a pocket-sized notebook and flipped through it. "I think we'll start with Mr....Del Rio," he said, pretending to read the name off one of the pages.

"I can't say I'm surprised," Polley said. "The Annies can't get enough of that one. Never seen so many skirts in the stands as I have since he was called up."

He pointed Guy and Dr. Happy toward one corner of the locker room, where Cam Del Rio was standing. Del Rio was laying out the pieces of his uniform on a bench next to his locker in what appeared to Guy to be some sort of game-day ritual. When they got closer Guy raised an eyebrow in surprise. Del Rio was even bigger in the flesh than he was in Blair's photograph.

"Cam Del Rio?" Dr. Happy spoke up.

Del Rio turned and smiled at the two. Despite his considerable muscle bulk, he retained a cherubic, fresh-faced countenance.

"How can I help you?" he drawled. Guy guessed the accent as Iowan.

"We're from the Centers for Disease Control," Dr. Happy said. "We're conducting a routine investigation in order to prevent a potential venereal disease epidemic."

"VD?" Del Rio shook his head and laughed. "I'm sure I don't know anything about that."

"I'm sure you don't," Dr. Happy said. "But we do have a protocol to follow." He showed Del Rio the photograph. "Have you had relations with this woman?"

Del Rio didn't even look at the picture. "A gentleman doesn't talk about such things, sir," he said.

"Look," Guy said, trying a friendlier tone. "I know you don't want to tell tales outside of school here, but this girl is in need of treatment. We need to find her whereabouts so we can help her."

"Sorry, gentlemen," Del Rio said. "But I wouldn't know anything about any wayward girls. And I surely don't know anything about getting VD."

"So no rashes?" Dr. Happy asked. "Lesions, discharge?"

Del Rio smiled as he adjusted his uniform on the changing bench. "Not a drop, sir."

As Del Rio leaned forward, Guy noticed something inside his

open locker. It was an orange prescription bottle, like the ones he had taken from Blair's hotel room. He squinted, trying to read the label, but couldn't make out the name of the drug.

"How about acne breakouts?" Dr. Happy asked. "Easy irritability?"

"I'm beginning to take offense to this interview, if that answers your question," Del Rio replied.

"And everything down there is operating properly?" Dr. Happy's eyes directed downward at Del Rio's jock strap.

"What are you implying?"

"These are all standard questions for this type of situation," Guy butt in, trying to sound reassuring. However, he was starting to second-guess Dr. Happy's interrogation technique. Del Rio's face was turning different shades of crimson, and Guy wanted to wrap things up before Del Rio got any more upset at them.

"I'm only going to tell you one more time." Del Rio took a small step toward Dr. Happy. "You're barking up the wrong tree. I suggest you beat it before this interview becomes hazardous to *your* health."

"Message received, Mr. Del Rio," Dr. Happy said. "I think we have enough to go on from here."

As they walked out of the stadium, Guy looked at Dr. Happy with disapproval. "Fine job with the cross-examination," he said. "You got stonewalled by a meathead kid from the sticks."

"No," Dr. Happy said. "We did just fine."

"What are you talking about? We got nothing."

Dr. Happy shook his head. "Did you catch a look inside the kid's locker?"

"What about it?"

"He's got a prescription bottle in it."

"Yeah, I saw it too."

"Did you make out what the prescription was for?"

Guy shook his head.

"Androstenedione," Dr. Happy said.

"What's that?"

"An androgen. Synthetic male sex hormones. And I caught a look at who the prescribing physician was. Do you have one of Blair's pill bottles?"

Guy produced one of the bottles from his hip pocket.

"Read the label," Dr. Happy instructed. "Is the prescriber a Dr. I. Constantine?"

Guy read the label on the bottle and nodded. "Who's Dr. Constantine?" he asked. "Do you know him?"

"Everyone knows him," Dr. Happy replied.

"Do you know where to find him?"

"Yes. His clinic will be closed by now. But in a couple of hours, he'll be holding office hours in a nightclub on Pico Boulevard."

Guy wrinkled his brow. "What kind of doctor sees patients in a nightclub?"

"The kind that caters to errant souls like your girlfriend and Mr. Baseball back there."

"You mean he's a croaker?" Guy asked.

Dr. Happy shook his head. "You're a croaker when you operate out of the back of a van in Van Nuys. When you have an office on Wilshire and drive a Rolls Royce, you don't call it that."

"What do you call it then?"

"He calls it concierge medicine."

# CHAPTER 17

The entrance to Club TechNoir was blocked by a velvet rope and guarded by a large Mediterranean bouncer, whose shaved arms were adorned in tattoos that advertised his time in both an elite military unit and a drug-trafficking biker gang. Even after Guy and Dr. Happy got to the front of the line, he looked through them like they were made of glass, waving younger, better-dressed partygoers in ahead of them. Finally growing tired of the cold shoulder, Dr. Happy pulled a roll of bills out of his pocket and showed it to the bouncer.

"We're here to spend money," he stated.

The bouncer gave them an up-and-down and then shook his head.

"Look Golden Girls," he growled. "We've met our quota for sausage for the night. You want to get in, you better find two pairs of tits to come in with you."

Dr. Happy turned around and looked at the group of teenage girls in line behind them. The blonde closest to them made a face like she just stepped in dog shit.

"Ew!" she gagged. "Like, don't look at us."

Guy engaged the bouncer. "I'm confused. You're insulting our manhood, yet you just implied that you stay home Saturday nights and watch Bea Arthur sitcoms."

The bouncer took a step closer to him.

Thinking quickly, Guy pulled out Rip's American Express card and held it out like it was a police badge. "What if we get bottle service?"

Without a word, the bouncer lifted the velvet rope.

Inside, the club was so dark it took several minutes for Guy's eyes to adjust. Then, as soon as they did, a powerful strobe light effect nearly blinded him. A deep bass beat reverberated through the club, amplified by the heavy footsteps of the partygoers dancing in time.

"I feel like Helen Keller in here," Guy said to Dr. Happy.

Dr. Happy maintained his default austere expression. Guy couldn't tell if Dr. Happy disapproved of the reference or just didn't hear him over the music. Dr. Happy leaned into Guy's ear and spoke clearly. "You check the bar. I'm going to see if he's in the bathroom."

Before Guy could ask why he would look for him *there*, Dr. Happy had disappeared into the crowd. On his own, Guy pushed his way through the club, past hyperkinetic Wall Street types licking their gums as they tried to keep the attention of blank-faced, iron-deficient models. He was having trouble locating the bar, so disoriented that he was only vaguely confident that the ceiling was above him and the floor beneath him. Wandering blindly through the crowd, Guy turned and bumped into a large, vaguely Lebanese-looking man in an Armani suit, wearing a pair of Ray-Bans. Guy thought the man was saying something to him, but he couldn't hear anything over the song blasting through the house speakers.

Guy kept moving. Feeling self-conscious, he half-heartedly stepped with the music. A thin redhead with sunken, dilated eyes noticed and walked up to him. Without speaking or making eye contact, she swayed in time with Guy, raising her arms above her head like a praying mantis.

Guy tried to step away but he was penned in by the other bodies on the dance floor. The redhead leaned in closer to him and his eyes caught the glint of a white residue circling one of her nostrils, like salt around the rim of a margarita glass. She smiled and Guy felt her hips brush against his.

Suddenly, an arm grabbed him by the shoulder, spinning him around.

"I didn't touch her," Guy blurted.

He found himself staring at Dr. Happy, who shook his head in response. "He's in the back," he stated. "Come on."

He led Guy to a private room, which was pushed back even further into the dark recesses of the nightclub and guarded by another velvet rope. Guy sighed.

Dr. Happy ignored him and turned to the new bouncer. "We're with the doctor."

"Prove it," the bouncer replied.

Dr. Happy pulled out one of the prescription bottles, the one containing amphetamines made out to Cam Del Rio, held it up to the bouncer, close enough for him to read the label. "You recognize his handiwork?" he asked.

The bouncer didn't say anything. But he didn't tell Dr. Happy to go to hell either.

"He sent me out for a delivery," Dr. Happy added. "He's going to want this."

The bouncer seemed to consider this for a moment, then he nodded and let them past. The VIP room was much less crowded, and of higher-class clientele. The women still looked anorexic, but without visible bruises or track marks. The men were all well-built, wearing linen suits and Gucci loafers like it was a uniform they all coordinated ahead of time. Guy wondered if any of them were ballplayers.

At the rear of the room, a plush couch was pushed back against the wall. Piled on top were more women than could comfortably fit, and in the middle of the action sat Immanuel Constantine, MD. He was dressed in the type of couture that occurs when people with absolutely no fashion sense have sudden access to dispensable income. His unnaturally dark hair and surgically taut face made it impossible to place his age any more accurately than somewhere north of forty. He was grinning madly and whispering into the ear of one of the girls on the couch with him.

He stopped as soon as he saw Dr. Happy approach. "Ah, the good doctor." Constantine beamed.

Guy squinted at him. "If he's the good doctor, what does that make you?"

Constantine smiled. "The better doctor."

Dr. Happy seemed unwounded by the comment. "I didn't come here to compare dick sizes."

"What did you come here to do?" Constantine offered a comical frown as he leaned back into the couch. "Talk trade? Swap goods?"

"How about we play truth or dare?" Guy interjected.

Constantine recoiled slightly and turned to Dr. Happy. "What is this, summer camp?" he asked before addressing Guy. "Seriously, truth or dare?"

"Seriously," Guy replied. "Like you tell us the truth about where we can find Blair Weston, and we don't dare tell the Medical Board of California what we just found in Cam Del Rio's locker."

Constantine's eyes lit up upon hearing Blair's name. "I'm sorry," he said. "We haven't met."

"That's right," Guy replied. "We haven't."

"Come on, don't be so unfriendly." He reached inside his sport coat and retrieved a business card, which he handed to Guy, stating: "I'm a good friend to have."

Guy read the business card. Under Constantine's name it simply said: "Doctor."

"That sounds legit," Guy mumbled.

"So." Constantine leaned in toward Guy. "How do you know Blair?"

Guy felt his skin get hot. "How do *you* know Blair?" he returned through gritted teeth.

Constantine shook his head condescendingly. "You're

overplaying your hand, gentlemen," he said. "I'm guessing what you really want to know is how *recently* have I known Blair."

Guy's jaw clenched.

"Hey." Dr. Happy maintained his calm tone of voice. "We just came here to find out where the girl is."

"You just interrupted a private party." Constantine's jovial expression suddenly turning sour. "You walked in here, uninvited, and started insinuating improprieties, with a decidedly inhospitable attitude that I do not appreciate."

"Look," Dr. Happy started.

"You look," Constantine interrupted. "*Doctor.* Your little house call has outworn its welcome and I think it's time you discharged yourselves from the premises." He leaned back against the couch. "Please, give my regards to the B-Listers in Toluca Lake. I'll call you next time I need someone to write a Valium prescription for my Bichon Frise."

Guy offered up a coy smile. "Talk about overplaying your hand. This guy's about as subtle as a Budd Dwyer press conference." He tapped Dr. Happy on the arm. "Let's go," Guy urged. "We'll ask him again after the indictment. He's sure to be in a more charitable mood then."

Constantine had been in the act of raising a Champagne glass to his lips when he paused. "Indictment?" he asked Guy. "What the fuck are you talking about?"

"I'm talking about the Controlled Substances Act," Guy replied. "And how even licensed physicians can be found guilty of distribution charges if a jury is convinced that the drugs were given irresponsibly." He took the prescription bottle from Dr. Happy and showed it to Constantine, making sure Del Rio's name on the label was visible. "You know, the LA DEA Office is only about twenty minutes from here."

Constantine's fingers tightened their grip around his Champagne flute. "Who *are* you?" His dark eyes shot a fiery glare at Guy.

"I bet every man and woman in this room has had a script

written by you," Guy continued. "But how many have them have actually been seen in your office? It would take about five seconds during discovery to figure that one out." He leaned in closer. "You want to know who I am? I'm the one thing you fear." He snatched the Champagne flute from Constantine's limp fingers and poured the contents down his throat. "I'm an attorney at law, asshole," Guy said. "Your goddamn kryptonite."

Constantine's eyes nervously shot to the bouncer in the doorway.

"How old is *she*?" Guy pointed the glass toward a particularly fresh-faced girl on Constantine's left. "Did he give you anything?" he asked her. Before she could reply, Guy handed Constantine back the empty Champagne flute, saying: "Your business card didn't say you were board certified in pediatrics."

"Okay," Constantine relented, taking back the glass in an automatic fashion. "You said you weren't here to compare dick sizes. So let's just fold up our cocks and talk like colleagues, okay?"

"Like doctors, lawyers, and Indian chiefs?" Dr. Happy asked.

"Yeah," Constantine replied. "But first let me get the squaws out of here."

He gestured for the girls to vacate the couch and signaled for Guy and Dr. Happy to sit down. Now with a closer view, Guy couldn't help but notice the subtle difference in color and texture between the hair on the sides of Constantine's head and that on top. Guy wondered if anything about this new acquaintance of his was on the up-and-up.

"All right, what do you want to know?" Constantine sputtered once the three of them were alone.

"Where's Blair?" Guy asked bluntly.

"I haven't seen Blair in days," Constantine answered. "And as you can see," he gestured to the abundance of female flesh in the room. "I'm not exactly broken-hearted over it."

"Is that unusual?" Dr. Happy asked. "To not hear from her for a few days?"

"She's what you might call a frequent flyer," Constantine replied. "It wasn't unusual for her to call me up several times a day."

"You seem really distraught about her disappearance," Dr. Happy remarked.

"If she's dead in a ditch somewhere," Constantine said with a very deliberate staccato intonation, a harsh acidity to his voice, "I'm not going to shed any tears."

"Unless she's dead from an OD on something you gave her," Guy countered. "That would amount to involuntary manslaughter."

"Only if the DA gave a shit enough about a tart like her to press charges," Constantine said. "Which is unlikely."

"When did she introduce you to Cam Del Rio?" Dr. Happy asked, changing the subject.

"Del Rio?" Constantine furrowed his brow, his expression telegraphing genuine ignorance. "What does he have to do with Blair?"

"She chases ballplayers and she's fucking you for drugs," Dr. Happy answered. "Del Rio's had a disappointing rookie year. Blair knows you can offer pharmaceutical enhancement. I figure she uses you to get brownie points with Del Rio, plus maybe get a commission for the referral."

Constantine shook his head. "Blair's no groupie. I don't know what she is. She defies diagnosis, that one. There isn't enough room in the DSM to define that amount of crazy."

"So how'd you get in with the ball club then?" Dr. Happy asked. "If Blair didn't provide the introduction."

"Let's just say I made friends with someone very well connected."

"Connected?" Guy looked at Dr. Happy. "Let me guess," he murmured, "Antonin Casparo."

Constantine sat up, his eyes narrowed on Guy. "How'd you know?"

"It was Casparo's idea for you to start writing for ballplayers?" Dr. Happy asked.

"A few months ago one of his guys calls me up," Constantine explained. "Says he was referred by one of my satisfied patients."

"You mean customers?" Guy remarked.

"He came to me with a business proposition," Constantine continued. "He asked if I wanted to branch out into sports medicine. Casparo apparently has a lot of product but needed medical expertise to make sure the boys are taking it properly. Mr. Del Rio was my first patient referred through this new venture."

"So Blair had nothing to do with you treating Del Rio?" Dr. Happy asked.

"No."

"But she found out about it," Guy said.

"What exactly are you two are doing here?" Constantine asked. His gaze again shot toward the bouncer, this time accompanied by a head jerk in Guy's direction. "What is Blair up to?"

"Never mind her," Guy said. "Do you know what you've gotten yourself into? Getting into bed with Casparo?"

Constantine pursed his lips. "All I know is that in this town it's all about who your friends are. If I turned Casparo down, then I'd have a pretty powerful enemy right now. But instead, I have a pretty powerful friend."

The bouncer was on his feet now, walking toward them. Guy continued his press on Constantine. "Casparo doesn't make friends. He collects people. Like a spoiled little girl collects dolls. And just like a spoiled little girl, when he gets tired of one of his dolls, he throws it away."

Dr. Happy motioned to Guy. "Come on. You're wasting your breath on this one. Look at him. He thinks he's going to live till the end of time."

"Then he'll be wishing for the end of time before too long," Guy said. He got to his feet just as the bouncer arrived. Without saying a word, the bouncer pushed Guy and Dr. Happy toward the exit. Guy complied, carefully walking backward, but Dr.

Happy stretched his neck and called out over the bouncer's shoulder to Constantine.

"One last question," he said. "It wasn't Bennies we saw in Del Rio's locker. It was an androgen. What are you trying to do? Turn the ball club into the East German women's swim team?"

"That was always your problem," Constantine called back. "You think too small." He smiled as the distance between them increased. Constantine then waved the girls back to the couch.

Guy watched as the women returned to their station, clambering over Constantine like bees to a hive. He realized there was no use in Dr. Happy responding at that point. If they were going to leave the club with their kneecaps intact, it was time to stop talking. And anyway, Constantine had already forgotten all about them.

# CHAPTER 18—March 15, 1986

Guy McCann had been unable to sleep in his apartment. Milloy wasn't answering his home phone, so Guy decided to spend the remainder of the night at the office, desperate to catch Milloy the instant he arrived at work the next morning. Guy's stomach was so twisted in knots that he had to keep pacing the hallway to distract himself from his abdominal pain. Finally, in the last minutes before the sun rose, he passed out on Milloy's desk, but when the doorknob turned, he woke up and bolted from his chair. Milloy hadn't entered the room before Guy started talking rapid-fire.

"Where have you been?" Guy shouted. Without taking a breath, he added: "Have you seen the Giardini brief?"

Milloy held an arm up between himself and Guy. "Take it easy," he said. "You look like you're about to have a coronary."

"Have you seen the brief?" Guy repeated. He pointed to the briefcase he had left resting on Milloy's desk.

Milloy sighed as he hung his jacket on the coat rack in the corner of the office. "Yeah, I read it," he replied. "What's the problem? It's cookie-cutter stuff. It should be right up your alley."

Guy looked at Milloy incredulously. "I'm sorry," he began, "but when did we start referring to rape charges as 'cookie-cutter stuff'?"

"Give me a break," Milloy said. "That's a bit of a reach. The

DA'd be lucky to get him on felony sexual battery. As it is, you'll probably be able to plea down to misdemeanor sexual assault." He motioned Guy out of his way and sat down in the chair behind his desk. "Haven't *you* read the brief?"

Guy flopped into a chair opposite Milloy's. "The girl was fifteen years old," Guy said.

"Yeah," Milloy replied. "And kids make for very unreliable testimony. It's so easy to get them to contradict themselves during cross-examination. Trust me, the DA does not want her on the stand."

Guy's mouth hung open. "Okay," he began. "That's pretty callous. Even for you."

Milloy folded his arms across his chest and assumed a soft-toned voice. "Look, we're not supposed to know about this, but the feds are pressing Giardini to turn state's evidence against Casparo in exchange for a lighter sentence. If you can't convince Giardini that you can avoid a felony conviction, he's going to roll over. I don't need to remind you that Casparo is a very important client. One that you do not want to disappoint."

"What if we get a postponement? Let this case cool off a bit. Maybe we can find another lawyer to defend him. Casparo won't care as long as this scumbag walks, right?"

"There is urgency here. Every day Giardini has these charges weighing on his shoulders is another day he has to consider the feds' offer."

"Even if I didn't care about how taking a case like this would make me look to the public," Guy said, "I don't think I could defend this scumbag and still look at myself in the mirror."

"Look, haven't you been paying attention to what I've been saying?" Milloy said. "The feds are already trying to get his sentence reduced in exchange for fingering Casparo. Even if you don't defend him, Giardini's still going to walk on this."

"And the DA's going to accept a deal?"

"The DA doesn't care about what happened to that girl. He's running for mayor next election. He only cares about the headline he's going to get for prosecuting Casparo." He leaned in over his desk toward Guy. "Are you telling me you'd rather be on that side of fence? Don't act so naïve. You know how this game works. There aren't any good guys in this one."

Guy hung his arms limply at his sides. "Did you look at the pictures the cops took?" he asked. "The ones from the hospital?"

"No," Milloy said. "I didn't."

Guy stood and opened his briefcase. From inside he pulled out a stack of four-by-six glossy photographs and tossed them across the desk to Milloy.

"You look at those and then tell me which side you want to be on."

Milloy kept his eyes pointed straight at Guy. "I don't need to see them," he said. "And you don't need to think about this anymore. It's out of your hands."

"That's what I'm getting at," Guy said. "Giardini doesn't need me on this. The arresting officers screwed this up. The search warrant has the wrong apartment number on it. The clothes they took from his place to match the fibers they found on the girl...that's the whole case right there. It's bullshit, but with the right judge that's enough to rule the evidence as inadmissible. Without that, the DA's got nothing to pin Giardini to the girl." Guy sighed and lowered his head into his hands. "This is a slam dunk," he continued. "Anyone can submit the motion to dismiss. It doesn't have to be me."

"That's what I'm talking about," Milloy insisted. "If Giardini's going to walk no matter what, then what does it matter if it's you or someone else getting the credit for it?"

Guy looked up from his hands until his eyes met Milloy's. "You still haven't looked at the pictures."

"I don't want to look at them."

"Look at them," Guy ordered. "Then I'll answer your question."

Milloy's gaze lowered to the desk. To the glossy photographs lying on top. He didn't look very long. "All right," he whispered after a brief pause. "I'll take care of it."

Guy's eyes brightened. "You mean it?" he asked. "You'll talk to Casparo?"

"It'll get it taken care of."


"Can't sleep?"

Guy shook his head as he sat up. He should have been exhausted given the events earlier that evening. The lovers' spat at the restaurant, precipitated by one too many bottles of wine, had escalated into a shouting match on the car ride home and culminated in them ripping each other's clothes off the second they crossed the threshold of his apartment. They had more or less fallen into this pattern in the last few months—knockdown drag outs that seamlessly transitioned to frenzied hate-fucking—and despite suffering minor injuries from both phases of the cycle, Guy had trouble complaining about it. The fighting just made their relationship feel more real to him, like they were a normal couple, and it helped him forget that Blair was still working for Anneleise Casparo. As for what followed the fighting, well, that juice was always worth the squeeze. But this particular evening, Guy was unable to summon any postcoital contentment as he turned restlessly under the sheets. Physically he felt depleted, but his mind wouldn't shut off.

He reached for the glass on the counter but found it empty. He sighed loudly before falling back onto his pillow. Blair rolled over so she was facing him. She narrowed her gaze at him, studying the lines on his face. She reached over with one hand and ran her fingers gingerly through the hair just above his left ear.

"Do you have a gray hair?" she asked, feigning astonishment.

He reflexively pulled his head away from her. "It wouldn't surprise me," he murmured.

She stuck out her bottom lip. "You need to stop thinking so much," she said. "You realize there is a well-accepted inverse correlation between awareness and misery, don't you?"

"If that were true, then wouldn't I be happier if you hadn't told me that?"

Blair rolled her eyes.

Guy shifted his weight so that he was propped up on his left elbow and turned to face Blair.

"I can't stop thinking about this Giardini case."

Blair frowned. "You said Milloy would take care of it."

"That's right, I said that," Guy said. "But you didn't seem too convinced when I said it before. And you don't seem any more convinced of it now."

"Can you trust him?" Blair asked.

"Milloy?" Guy considered. "As much as I can trust anyone."

"Can you trust anyone?"

"I trust you," Guy answered.

"Yeah." Blair sighed, lying back onto the bed, a disappointed expression on her face as if Guy had just given a wrong answer. After several seconds she turned her head toward Guy and asked him: "What you need is leverage."

Guy's brow wrinkled. "Leverage against what?"

Blair rolled back over so her body was facing Guy again. "Casparo's not the kind of guy who likes being told what to do," she began. "If he wants you on that trial and you say no, then you're going to have a problem. The leverage is how you solve that problem."

Guy looked at her. "What do you have in mind? Do you have something on Casparo?"

"Maybe, but I'm not totally sure what it is yet," Blair said. "Let's put a pin in it for the time being. I'd rather give it to you all at once than hand you something small right now that might end up being nothing."

"Are you being serious?"

"Just hang on a little longer and no matter what Milloy promises you, don't make any waves with Casparo until I get you the whole story. Then you've got your leverage."

Guy threw her an incredulous grin. "And you'd do all that

for little old me?"

"Well, I can't do it all by myself. I might be able to get some intel on Casparo, but the word of a working girl doesn't go too far in this town." She widened her eyes and batted her lashes at him. "Now, an attorney-at-law on the other hand…"

"You mean, you dig the dirt and I cut the deal?"

"Seems like a reasonable arrangement," Blair answered. "You wash my back and I wash yours. And just maybe we both stay clean for good after that."

*If only it was that simple.* Blair certainly had been around the block, but what she was talking about seemed way above her paygrade. *Better leave this to the professionals,* he said to himself, thinking about his meeting with Milloy. But Guy didn't want to upset Blair. He lacked the stamina for either another argument or another round of make-up sex, let alone both. So he decided to humor her instead.

"If you were to find something, some leverage," Guy began, "you could be putting yourself in a very dangerous position."

Blair smirked. "I know how to take care of myself."

"I don't doubt that," Guy said. "But if you get your hands on something, when you do, you might need to lay low for a while. Until I can make the deal."

"Like I said," Blair countered. "I know how to take care of myself."

"Yeah, but how will I find you afterwards?"

Blair shook her head. "Call me crazy," she began, "but I think that's the least of your worries."

"You're crazy," Guy fired back, grinning ear to ear. "And I disagree. I think finding you is going to be the first."

Blair batted her eyelashes playfully. "If you want me, you'll find me. If I want you, I'll be found." She pushed Guy back onto the bed and laid her head softly against his chest.

That sounded good enough for Guy, at least for the night. He closed his eyes and after a few minutes he was able to fall asleep.

* * *

Guy woke up to the phone ringing. He leapt out of bed and lifted the receiver off the hook before the second ring.

"I've got a status update," Milloy informed him.

"Yeah." Guy kept his voice low, looking back over at the bed.

"We should meet to go over this in person. Get organized. Can you come now?"

"At the office?"

"No." There was a pause. "Can you come to the old building?"

Guy's forehead wrinkled. "Why?"

"I'm there now. I had to pick up a couple things."

"You still had a key?"

"Yeah, don't worry about it." Milloy's voice started to sound urgent. "Come around the back entrance, I'll let you in."

Guy hung up the phone and looked at the bed again. Underneath the covers, Blair slept soundly. Although unconscious, the corner of her mouth was upturned, as if she were smiling. Guy considered waking her up to say goodbye, but then decided against it.


Thirty minutes later, Milloy greeted Guy at the rear stair entrance of the office building their practice had occupied until a month prior. Climbing up the stairs to the second floor that housed their former offices, Guy reflected on the excitement he experienced when they moved from the modest, dated building—with its pea green and saffron wallpaper and faded orange polypropylene furniture—to the smooth glass and chrome-clad offices where they presently resided. Milloy was noticeably reserved. The time it took for them to walk up the stairs was the longest Guy could recall Milloy going without talking.

They arrived at Milloy's former office. His old, battered desk sat in the corner, its plastic-over-chipboard top and dented enameled metal body appearing even more pathetic without any additional furniture in the room. The carpet was worn and pulled up in the corners, as if the whole space was going to be stripped down to the studs once they left.

Guy pointed at the desk. "Don't tell me you came back here for that. I don't think that's the image we're trying to project these days."

"Don't worry about that," Milloy said. His head swiveled about the room with a disconcerting amount of energy. Guy noticed the sweat beading up on his upper lip.

"What's going on?" Guy inquired.

"Look," Milloy began, "I told you I'd take care of things. And in a way, things are being taken care of."

"What are you talking about?"

"It just might not be taken care of the way we had hoped," Milloy continued.

"What did you do?" Guy took a step backward. "What's going on?"

"It's just that..."

"It's just what?"

A voice boomed into the room, answering the question. "It's that he can't bring himself to give you the bad news."

Guy turned and saw Casparo walk in, flanked by the well-tanned gunman that had accompanied Guy and Milloy in the car ride back from their first meeting with Casparo. Guy felt the same chill run down his spine when the gunman entered. His gaze was centered on Guy, bearing down on him in a way that made Guy feel small and insecure.

"I understand that you are experiencing cold feet about defending my associate, Mr. Giardini," Casparo said.

"Mr. Casparo." Guy's voice containing a slight tremble. "I wasn't going to..."

"Are you having cold feet, Mr. McCann?" Casparo asked.

Guy looked over and Milloy. Milloy did not look back at him.

"Mr. Casparo," Guy continued, "I swear that I..."

"Answer the question, Counselor," Casparo interrupted again.

Not knowing how else to respond, Guy nodded feebly.

"Well, then," Casparo replied, "we'll just have to warm them for you." He turned back to the gunman at his side. "Rip, if you would please."

Rip reached into his sport coat and produced an Italian stiletto switchblade. He depressed the button on the knife's handle and the blade sprang out into place. He took a step closer to Guy and held the knife up to his face, as if inviting Guy to admire the spear tip blade. Guy took a deep breath and held it.

Rip then pivoted and thrust the knife into Milloy's gut, driving in the blade all the way to the hilt. Milloy's eyes widened and his mouth opened as if he was going to gasp in shock, but no noise came out. Rip pulled the knife upward with a smooth, violent jerking motion, slicing open Milloy's abdominal wall and causing his intestines to spill out onto the floor with the spring-loaded action of a jack-in-the-box.

Guy went numb. His sudden sense of dissociation was so extreme that he had only the vaguest awareness of the warm stream of urine running down his leg.

Milloy's body fell forward onto the soiled carpet. Rip produced a handkerchief from his coat pocket and began methodically cleaning his hands and switchblade.

Casparo stepped forward to Guy and said: "I want to you realize something. Everything has happened for a reason." He cocked his head and looked at Guy like he was scolding a child who had just said his first naughty word. "And you know it. You just don't want to admit it to yourself."

He started pacing around Guy, whose inability to move suggested the appearance of a soldier at attention.

"All those trials you won," Casparo continued. "You want to think it was because you're such a smart guy. It couldn't be possible that the judges who kept agreeing with your motions, the inept prosecutors who kept shooting themselves in the feet, that they all had some kind of conflict of interest. You're really just that good a lawyer, right?"

Guy was silent. In the corner of his vision he could make out Milloy's lifeless form, lying immobile in the middle of a slowly expanding circle of blood. He saw, but he could not react.

"Don't delude yourself into thinking that anyone other than me is in charge here," Casparo went on. "You take the cases I give you. You defend the clients I tell you to. And if I get the idea that you're not putting one hundred percent of your effort in defending me and my associates, I might just tip off the California bar association about your relationship with Ms. Weston. They disbar lawyers for defending clients in exchange for sex. The state supreme court has set what you would call a precedent for that."

At the mention of Blair, Guy felt out of breath. He couldn't feel the floor under his feet, but he could feel his chest rapidly expand and contract.

"And that's not all," Casparo continued. He looked over at Rip, who responded with an understanding nod of his head. Rip produced a leather attaché case, opened it, and produced three reams of paper, which he placed in separate stacks on the desk. Casparo then reached into the breast pocket of his overcoat and produced a fountain pen.

"What's this?" Guy was surprised he could get the words out.

Casparo led Guy to the desk and motioned toward the first stack of papers. "This appoints you as my designee in several pending financial transactions. For various reasons it would be best if these transactions are not made in my name." He then pointed to the second set of papers. "This one takes the proceeds that you earn as a result of these transactions and places them into a trust."

"A trust?" Guy asked. "You mean, your trust?"

"Again, not in my name," Casparo clarified. "But for all intents and purposes...well, let's just say that you don't need to worry about all that extra money going to your head."

Behind him, Rip chortled. Guy looked up and saw Rip licking his lips.

"The third is a life insurance policy in your name," Casparo continued. "The policy appoints me as the sole beneficiary." He held the fountain pen out for Guy to take. "You will now sign the papers."

Guy's eyes focused on the tip of the fountain pen. Its beveled edge was saturated with ink, and Guy silently watched as a single drop fell onto the carpet.

"Once you sign the policy," Casparo concluded, "your death will be worth a substantial amount of money to me. You should keep that in mind before you get any more delusions of independence. You should also keep that in mind as a motivating factor in your obligation to me as my attorney. Alive, you are only worth to me what you accomplish in the courtroom. Anything short of a stellar legal defense record will be viewed as an unfavorable cost-benefit ratio in keeping you alive. You might also consider that a slow, painful death will pay out no fewer dollars than a quick and merciful one."

Guy didn't remember taking the pen, or signing the papers, or leaving the office building. He did remember racing back to his apartment, the panic in his stomach, only to find that Blair was already gone. He wanted to think that she had just left on her own, having grown impatient waiting for him to return. But the broken glass in the corner and the upturned nightstand in the bedroom told him otherwise. A sudden realization hit him and the panic in his gut was replaced by a dullness, an emptiness. He walked outside and stepped into his car, no destination in mind. He didn't feel the gas pedal as his foot pushed it to the floorboards, nor did he feel the grip of the steering wheel as he guided the Datsun 300ZX onto the street. It wasn't until he was hundreds of miles away that the sensation started to return to his body. And even then, all he felt was the hot, dry desert air. He tried not to think about time after that. He tried not to count the days he was living as a dead man, all alone, with no point of reference to tell him which direction he was headed in. If he was headed anywhere at all.

# CHAPTER 19—October 2, 1987

Guy was sitting alone in the diner booth, waiting for Dr. Happy to return from the row of pay phones in the back. He looked down at the murky liquid in his coffee cup, its roasted flavor replaced with a scorched bitterness. Guy poured creamer from its single-serve container into his cup until the contents turned a more pleasant auburn color. He raised the cup to his lips, took a swallow, and winced. The cream had improved the appearance, but the coffee still tasted like shit.

When Dr. Happy appeared, Guy shot a baleful glare at him.

"Jeez, you're not a morning person, are you?" Dr. Happy asked, taking his seat at the booth.

"We're moving in the wrong direction," Guy said. "You keep talking about going to places where Blair's already been. First we go back to the hospital, and where does that lead us? To Casparo. Then we find Del Rio, and then Constantine. And where do they lead us? To Casparo."

"Yeah."

"I don't want to find Casparo." Guy smacked a palm down on the table. "I want to stay as far away from that asshole as possible. I want to find Blair."

Dr. Happy placed his elbows on the table and rested his chin on top of his interlocked fingers. "I just got off the phone with a contact of mine who's crossed paths with Constantine a couple

of times. Apparently Constantine keeps a condo in Westwood."
Dr. Happy raised a knowing eyebrow. "For frequent flyers.
Some of them he lets have a key."

"Well, that's more like it. Did you get an address?"

"No," Dr. Happy answered. "And my guy didn't think the
phone number was listed."

Guy considered the options. "We can go to the county clerk's
office and pull the record of sale on the condo," he suggested.

Dr. Happy looked out the window next to them, trying to
get an indication of how traffic was moving. "I guess we're
heading downtown," he said.

"No, the Real Estate Records office is in Norwalk," Guy
said. "Hope you're in the mood for a drive."

Dr. Happy wrinkled his face for a moment before relaxing
his features and returning to his usual state of calm. "A lead's a
lead."

Dr. Happy threw a few bills onto the counter and they both
stood up and headed for the exit. The two walked outside to
parking lot where the Jaguar stood waiting for them. This time,
Dr. Happy automatically headed for the passenger side. Guy
paused for a second as he noticed this but kept silent as he
opened the driver's side door and slid behind the steering wheel.

Highway 101 was clogged with traffic, keeping the Jaguar in
low gear until they reached the Santa Ana Freeway. When Guy
turned on the car stereo to break the silence, the DJ was talking
about a brokerage firm indicted for laundering money for the
mob before he segued into "What You Need" by INXS. Growing
tired of the monotony of stop-and-go gridlock, Guy once again
desperately attempted conversation with Dr. Happy.

"What kind of doctor were you?" He then clarified: "Before
Casparo turned you into what you are now, I mean."

Dr. Happy kept looking straight out the windshield. "Casparo
didn't turn me into anything. I don't blame anyone but myself
for where I am right now."

"So how did you end up where you are now?" Guy asked.

"You didn't start out with aspirations of hotel room surgery and nightclub pharmacology?"

"I started out like everyone else," Dr. Happy replied. "Every medical student starts out with the same superhero fantasy. Getting paid to save lives. Be loved for a living. You grow up watching Ben Casey and you think that your future's going to be nothing but perky nurses and appreciative patients. Walk into any medical school on the first day of classes and look at their faces. First-years look like a bunch of Moonies. What they don't tell you is how little of your soul you'll have left by the time you come out the other end."

"Come on," Guy scoffed. "You're being a little melodramatic, don't you think? It can't be any different than what happens in law school. Medicine doesn't have a monopoly on disenfranchisement."

"You think so?" Dr. Happy asked. "You tell me if anything like this every happened to you in law school." He slid down in his seat, rolling his shoulders back a little before he began. "My first year out of medical school I was doing a medicine internship at a pretty big university hospital. I was rotating on the heme-onc inpatient service, and one night when I was on call, I was assigned to this liver cancer patient. He was end-stage, pretty bad shape. When I first saw him, I thought he was Indian or Middle Eastern or something and I couldn't figure out why he had an Irish last name. Later I realized that he actually was Irish. He was just so jaundiced it had turned his skin brown."

"All right," Guy said. "So?"

"The guy's doctor wanted him admitted because he had stopped eating," Dr. Happy continued. "He wanted him in the hospital to get rehydrated, intravenously. So basically, my only job was to get an IV in him. But I couldn't find a vein to save my life. He was so dry they had all collapsed. No matter where I stuck him, I couldn't strike blood. Making matters worse, he kept belching in my face as I was trying to place the IV."

"Okay, that's pretty gross," Guy conceded. "But that's not

that big a deal."

"There was something about his breath," Dr. Happy added. "His breath smelled...ungodly...this foul, bilious, feculent stench. He kept apologizing every time he did it, but he couldn't stop doing it. Just belching right in my face, one right after another. It got to the point where I started getting really pissed off at him. I couldn't concentrate on getting in the IV with him blowing that rank, sour breath in my face. So finally, I just snapped. I looked up at him and yelled, 'Knock it the fuck off!' I said it without even realizing I had said it."

Guy nodded, indicating to Dr. Happy that he was still listening as he turned the wheel and pulled the Jaguar onto the onramp for Highway 5.

"I instantly freaked out," Dr. Happy went on. "I couldn't believe I had just said that to a patient, and I looked at him really apologetically, saying 'I'm so sorry, I didn't mean that.' But he didn't say anything. He was just lying there, totally still."

Dr. Happy paused and turned his gaze away from Guy and looked passively out the passenger window.

"And then I realized why he wasn't saying anything." Dr. Happy's words came out plainly, devoid of emotion. "He didn't have a pulse. He had just died on me right then and there." He slowly exhaled through pursed lips before he continued. "So at this point I really started to freak out. I yelled for the nurse to call a code and, without even thinking about it, I leaned over his body and started doing chest compressions, you know, CPR. *One, two, three, four,* all the time yelling for the nurse to bring the crash cart. The nurse came in, and I kept doing the chest compressions, *five, six, seven, eight,* and I shouted at the nurse to start bagging him, to give him oxygen. And the nurse was there in the doorway, and behind her were two more nurses, and then the code team arrived. But they were all just standing there, looking at me with their mouths hanging open. And I looked over at them, still doing the compressions, starting to get pissed off. And in between compressions I shouted, 'What the fuck are you waiting for?'"

Dr. Happy picked at his lower lip.

"And then I looked down at the patient and I realized why they weren't doing anything," he said.

Guy became aware that his hands had been gripping tighter on the steering wheel. "Why weren't they?"

"The patient," Dr. Happy began. "His mouth. This...thick liquid was pouring out of his mouth. It was the consistency of mud and as black as tarmac. It was pumping out of his mouth with my chest compressions. Every time I pushed on his sternum, more of this stuff oozed out, like toothpaste out of a tube. It was pouring out onto the bed and spilling over the side down the front of my body."

Guy swallowed. "What was it?"

Dr. Happy exhaled. "It was fecal matter."

Guy did a double take. "Wait." He tried to digest what Dr. Happy had just said. "You mean shit?"

"Yes," Dr. Happy replied. "Shit."

"How...?"

"He had a bowel obstruction." Dr. Happy said it matter-of-fact, like he was describing the weather. "The cancer had spread to his colon and blocked it off. So everything just backed up inside him until he was packed full. And there was nowhere for any of it to go but up. Once it got to the top, it went back down into his lungs and put him in respiratory arrest. And when I was doing chest compressions, I was just pumping it all out, like I was squeezing a pair of bellows, through his mouth, the only way it could come out. It was all over my scrubs. I could feel it filling up my shoes, soaking through my socks and in between my toes. But I couldn't stop what I was doing. I had to keep giving him CPR. I had to keep trying to bring him back. And every time I pushed on his chest to force more blood through his body, more of this stuff gushed out all over me."

Guy blinked twice. "So, what happened?" he asked. "Did you bring him back?"

"The code team snapped out of it and ran in to help out." Dr. Happy seemed indifferent to Guy's reaction, like he was telling the story to himself more than to Guy. "A nurse suctioned out his mouth and one of the other interns was able to get a tube down his nose into his stomach so they could suck the rest of the stuff out and keep it from getting all over the place. We threw the kitchen sink at him: epi, atropine, this one maniac intern wanted to stick a needle in his heart in case he was in tamponade. But after about twenty minutes the code leader called it. By that time, I was covered head to toe in the guy's liquid shit, soaked with sweat, my arms ready to fall off, barely able to breathe. And he was gone."

A few seconds passed before Guy was able to speak again. "What happened next?" he asked. He was starting to feel light-headed.

"Nothing," Dr. Happy answered. He sat himself back up in seat. "That's my point. All that happened next was that the chief resident sent me to the call room to take a shower and change into clean scrubs. And by the time I got back to the unit, the nurses had washed the guy off. He was lying peacefully in bed, eyes closed, hair combed. You would have thought he was just sleeping. Then we broke the news to his wife, and she wasn't upset about it at all. He had been dying for months, so she was just glad he had passed so quickly. Within an hour, everyone was back to work, like nothing had happened." He turned so that he was looking straight at Guy's profile. "It was like nothing had happened," he repeated. "I squeezed two gallons of liquid shit out of a dead man's body and as far as anyone else was concerned, it was just another night in the hospital."

Guy slowed the Jaguar as they approached the bumper-to-bumper downtown traffic. After bringing the car to a stop at a red light, he turned to Dr. Happy and asked: "Was that the worst thing you've ever seen as a doctor?"

"Haven't you been paying attention?" Dr. Happy shot Guy a patronizing look before turning his gaze back to the traffic in front of them. "That was just the beginning."


Once Guy pulled the Jaguar off Imperial Highway and into the parking lot, Dr. Happy turned to him. "So, what's the plan?" he asked. He seemed to have already forgotten about his cancer patient story.

They got out of the car. "The plan for what?" he asked.

Dr. Happy followed him out of the car and through the parking lot toward the LA County Clerk's Office. "The plan to get Constantine's record of sale," he replied. "We can't just walk into town hall and ask for it, can we?"

"Of course we can." Guy was somewhat surprised by Dr. Happy's naiveté in the matter. "Except we're not walking into town hall. We're walking into the Public Information Office."

"And they're going to just hand that over?"

Guy stopped his stride and turned to Dr. Happy. "It's *public information*," he said. "If I want to, while I'm in there I could look up any action the state medical board has taken on you."

Dr. Happy just looked at Guy blankly.

"Your tax dollars at work," Guy said. "But since we're on a bit of a time crunch, I think I'll stick to checking up on one doctor at a time."

They walked into the building and headed for the Real Estate Records office. Inside, they found a bored-looking county registrar who barely acknowledged Guy and Dr. Happy when they entered.

"Record search?" she asked, tapping a set of fake nails against the surface of her desk.

"Correct," Guy answered.

"You know the year the property was sold?" she asked.

Guy shook his head. "No, just the owner's name. It's a condominium though."

The registrar frowned. "The records are indexed by name and year. I'll need at least a range of years in order to do the search."

"How about checking the last five years?" Guy asked.

By her facial expression, Guy might as well have suggested she deliver the records via her anus. "It'll be fifty cents per year for the search," she said. "That's nonrefundable."

Guy reached for the change in his pants pocket. "I think we might just be able to float that."

After several minutes, which Guy and Dr. Happy spent silently sitting in uncomfortable, plastic-backed, steel-framed chairs, the registrar returned with a stack of folders.

"I have two different sales during that time frame." She handed the folders to Guy. "You can make copies here if you want, but you can't take these with you. Copies are five cents a page."

Guy opened his folder and looked over the record of sale. "This one's in Westwood Village."

"This one's in Wilshire Center," Dr. Happy said, inspecting the folder in his hands.

"Yours is on the way back to the motel," Guy said. "How about we split up? I drop you off and then head to Westwood to check this one out. You find any sign of Blair, you leave a message with the motel front desk. Then stay by the phone in your room. I'll check in before dark."

"Sounds reasonable." Dr. Happy rubbed his tongue along his lower lip and tapped at the folder he was holding. "What do we do if one of us runs into Constantine instead?"

Guy considered. "Put him out of his misery," was his answer.

# CHAPTER 20

With Constantine's addresses in hand, Guy found the drive
back into the city more anxiety-provoking than the drive to
Norwalk, even without any anecdotes about cancer patients
shitting out of their mouths. Navigating the traffic toward
Wilshire Center was maddening for him, as every near miss with
a careless driver represented a potential delay in arriving at his
destination. When the Jaguar pulled in front of the condominium
complex on South Kingsley Drive, Dr. Happy exited the car,
nodded to Guy, and walked toward the building. Guy watched
him enter and paused before putting the Jaguar back in gear. He
reflected on how just twenty-four hours prior, technically
speaking, Dr. Happy had voluntarily killed him. And now he
was trusting Dr. Happy with Blair's life. Guy clenched his jaw
hard and then decided not to think about it any further. He
stepped on the gas pedal and drove to Westwood.

When he arrived, the door to Constantine's condominium
apartment was firmly locked. However, Guy found a window
that had been left ajar. After prying the screen away from the
frame, he was able to slide the window open enough to fit
through.

Once inside, Guy paced through the apartment. The lights
were off and there were no visible signs that anyone had recently
been living there. Guy carefully stepped along the bare wood

floors, trying to minimize the sounds of his footsteps. He reached a lofted bedroom and climbed the steps inside. The walls were adorned with framed Patrick Nagel prints. Otherwise, the room was sparsely decorated. Near the king-sized bed, which had not been slept in, was a nightstand with a bottle of perfume perched on top. Guy picked up the bottle and unscrewed the top. As he brought the bottle to his nose, he dropped the cap, causing it to bounce furiously on the hardwood floor, the noise echoing through the otherwise silent apartment. He dove to his knees and chased the perfume bottle cap as it rolled mischievously along the floor, coming to a rest in the corner of the bedroom. Guy picked up the bottle cap and upon rising hit his head on the lower edge of one of the framed posters, knocking it off the wall and causing it to crash down at his feet. Before he could react, Guy heard a giggle behind him.

He turned and found Blair standing at the top of the stairs, with a pathetic smile on her face.

"You know, Counselor," she said. "If you're here without a warrant, anything you find is inadmissible in court."

"I only came here for one thing," Guy said, straightening himself up.

"Let me guess." Blair's smile widened. "To run into inanimate objects and chew bubble gum." Her voice adopted a husky, mock-tough guy tone. "*And you're all out of bubble gum.*"

"Funny. But you know why I'm here."

"I suppose I do," Blair said. "When did you get back in town?"

"Three days ago. Your sister called me."

This elicited a giggle from Blair. "How is big sis, by the way?"

"Disproving any notion that loving Jesus can cure obesity, teenage apathy, or general malaise." Guy took a few steps toward her. "She's also in need of a sedative. You really got her wound up the other night."

Blair shrugged. "Big sisters are supposed to worry. That's their job."

"She thinks you've gone full loco this time," Guy stated. "Seems to be the consensus around town."

Blair raised an eyebrow. "It's not crazy if they're really out to get you."

"It is if you did something to make them."

"Well, after you pulled your disappearing act, I had to do something with my time," Blair said demurely. "And you know what they say about idle hands."

"It appears that your hands have been anything but idle," Guy said. "I was in your hotel room and found the drugs you left there. I met your new friend Constantine and I know this is his apartment. I know what kind of currency he trades in."

"You were in my hotel room?" Blair asked. She slunk toward him, still maintaining some distance between them but closing the gap. "You found my stash?" She took on a fake expression of astonishment. "*I swear it's not mine, Daddy. I was just holding it for a friend.*" Her voice grew slightly more serious. "Do you still have it on you?"

"Dr. Happy has it."

Blair's hands found their way to her hips. "I'm sorry? Who is Dr. Happy?"

"He's my..." Guy began, "my doctor. He works for Casparo. Well, he used to work for Casparo. He's been helping me track you down."

"Helping you? Why?"

"He thinks you might have something on Casparo. He's interested in early retirement but wants to avoid Casparo's usual severance package."

"A doctor, huh?" Blair's gaze became vacant for a second and Guy thought he lost her until she suddenly snapped back to him. "And what do you think?"

"I think you should get in the car with me right now and we drive as fast and as far as possible."

Blair's arms fell loose to her sides and she inched away from him. "That's what I thought you'd say. If only that offer was anywhere near as enticing as you think it sounds."

She started to turn for the door but Guy rushed over to flank her. "I don't want to play any more games, Blair," he said. "Whatever's going on with you, I want to know. Fuck that Constantine asshole. I want to hear it from you."

Blair laughed loudly. "From what I remember, you were never interested in hearing anything other than the sound of your own voice or seeing anything other than your reflection in the doe eyes of some helpless damsel in distress."

"And from what I remember, you're the one who couldn't leave the house without trouble following her and I was the one with the noose around his neck for keeping you out of prison."

Blair scowled. "You've built yourself up like quite the knight in shining armor considering how quickly you tucked your tail once things got a little hot."

"What choice did I have?" His voice raised to a shout. "They had everything on me. They had my license, my practice, my life." His tone softened. "They had you."

"No, Guy," Blair clarified. "They never had me. No one ever has, and no one ever will."

"No one?"

"That's right," Blair replied, stepping up to Guy. "No one." She lifted a hand to his face but her touch lacked delicacy. Instead, her fingers lingered on his healing black eye and Guy could see the disappointment in her eyes. "And if you think that you showing up here like some slow-witted comic book hero—whose super-power apparently is throwing his face in the path of other people's fists—is going to change that, then think again, because, as you can see, my knees have yet to go weak with adulation."

"Yeah, well we'll see about that."

Guy reached out and grabbed Blair by the waist, pulling her toward him suddenly. As she arrived in his grasp, he leaned his face toward hers. Blair then swung forward with the open palm of her right hand and slapped him across the face.

Guy pulled his head back in shock. He felt his face grow red hot and his teeth bare down onto each other as he clenched his jaw shut with rage. Guy grabbed Blair by the arm and threw her face down on the bed. She started to get up and he pushed her back down, pinning her to the bed with his weight. With his free hand he started unbuckling his belt.

"Wait," Blair cried out. "Stop!"

Her cry startled him back to reality. He relaxed his grip and let her go.

Blair stood up and turned to Guy, an astonished look on her face. She slowly walked away from him to the corner of the room. She paused next to the dresser and reached over to the turntable, carefully lifting the dust cover before removing the record from the platter mat. While Guy watched in confusion, she flipped through a stack of LPs next to the record player and stopped when she got to Duran Duran's *Rio*. Blair removed the record from the sleeve and placed Side 2 on the turntable. She set the needle on the third track and then, as the music began playing through the stereo speakers, walked back to the bed. Blair then bent over, placing her face sideways down against the bedspread, returning to the same position Guy had held her in moments earlier.

"Okay," Blair said softly as Simon Le Bon's vocals filled the room. "Now you can go ahead."

Guy took a deep breath. His rage had dissipated and was now replaced with only exasperation.

"Why are you always trying to make me crazy?" he asked.

Blair stood up and turned so she was facing him.

"Because," she murmured, reaching her arms around his neck, "I don't like doing anything by myself."

Guy felt her lips meet his. His fists clenched for a brief second. Then he let go.


After Dr. Happy watched Guy take off down South Kingsley Drive, he felt a sense of relief blow through him to complement the evening breeze. It wasn't so much that he wanted to be free of Guy's company. He just had a feeling that he was about to perform the kind of work that he preferred to do alone. He gripped his black medical bag, the handheld one he never left home without, and started up the concrete path into the development.

As he approached Constantine's Wilshire Center condo, Dr. Happy noted that the interior lights were on. He paused and knelt on the porch, checking the inventory of his medical bag. He then rose, leaving the bag on the porch off to the side, and gave the door a firm knock. A few seconds later the light behind the peephole disappeared. Dr. Happy took a step backward and stood squarely before the door, allowing whoever was gazing through the hole a full-frontal view of him. The door opened a crack and Dr. Happy saw a sliver of Immanuel Constantine's head appear in the opening. The light from the outdoor fixture reflected off his bald crown—Constantine had removed his toupee for the night.

"What are you doing here?"

Dr. Happy felt no need for small talk. "I'm looking for Blair."

"She's not here."

"I know she's not here," Dr. Happy said. "If you put that chinchilla you wear on your head back in its cage, then that means you're the only one here. I know it's just you and me."

"Not for long," Constantine growled. He opened the door wide enough to reach his arm out to Dr. Happy, showing off the cordless phone in his hand. Dr. Happy saw he was wearing a pair of silk pajamas under an ornate kimono. He detected gin on his breath.

"Are you going to call the cops?"

"No. I'm going to call my new friend Mr. Casparo and ask him to send some of his boys over to teach you a lesson about respecting others' privacy."

Dr. Happy put his hands in his jacket pockets and rocked back and forth on his heels. "This would be a lot easier if you would just let me in so we can talk like reasonable adults."

Constantine pointed his phone hand at Dr. Happy, wielding the extended metal antenna like a fencing saber. "Take another step, you cut-rate horse doctor, and I make the call."

Dr. Happy's eyes converged on the tip of the cordless phone antenna. "Then I guess we're doing this the hard way." Before Dr. Happy finished the sentence, the hypodermic needle was out of his pocket and his arm was arcing in an underhand motion. Constantine didn't have time to react before the needle punctured the fabric of his pajama pants and drove to the hilt into his thigh muscle. Constantine gasped as Dr. Happy depressed the plunger, then his knees started to buckle. Dr. Happy let go of the syringe and brushed past Constantine, crossing through the foyer to the kitchen, leaving Constantine to fumble weakly for the syringe. Dr. Happy returned with a chair and placed it behind Constantine, whose hands had found the syringe but couldn't muster the fine motor coordination required to remove it. Dr. Happy gently pushed him back into the chair, then closed and locked the front door.

Constantine strained to keep his head raised. The rage in his face trickled away and his breathing slowed into a steady rate. "Sodium thiopental?" he asked.

"Yes."

"A little old-fashioned, don't you think?" Constantine's speech had already started to slur. "I would have preferred Versed. Less of a hangover afterwards."

"That's the least of your worries." Dr. Happy checked his watch and pressed his index and middle fingers against Constantine's carotid artery. "Okay, are you comfortable?"

Constantine's eyelids drooped like window shades.

Dr. Happy was satisfied. "Good. Where's Blair?"

"I don't know." Constantine's head fell forward, his facial muscles so relaxed that jowls formed under either side of his chin, slowly flapping when he talked. "She comes and goes as she pleases."

"Does Anneleise know she's working you on the side?"

"Who's Anneleise?"

Dr. Happy brought his fingers under Constantin's chin and lifted his head. "Casparo's wife. She runs the prostitution racket for Casparo's syndicate."

"That sounds like unusual work for a mafia bride."

"Apparently she made her bones before they met." Dr. Happy said. "They're the syndicate's first supercouple."

"Like Luke and Laura?" Constantine asked. "How progressive."

Dr. Happy reminded himself that the Pentothal wouldn't last long. He had to stay on topic. "So the Casparos don't know that you and Blair were sleeping together?"

"I may have exaggerated my relationship with her," Constantine said. He struggled to curl up his lips into a sheepish grin. "Your friend was acting very rude the other night and I found it quite bothersome. I wanted to bother him back and it was obvious he has a past with Blair."

"He thinks he has a future with her."

Constantine stopped trying to smile. "Not likely."

Dr. Happy didn't argue the point. "So, you're not sleeping with her?"

"Blair? No."

"But you prescribed her lithium, gave her cocaine."

"I never gave her cocaine."

"But you prescribed her lithium."

"Mmff."

"What?" Dr. Happy used a thumb to pry open one of Constantine's eyes only to find the pupil rolled upward. Constantine was making a soft croaking sound with each breath.

Dr. Happy had guessed Constantine's weight when he filled the syringe, trying to estimate a dose large enough to be efficacious but not enough to completely anesthetize him. He had known there was a margin of error involved. He could just wait until the Pentothal wore off a little, but he didn't want to spend a second longer in the condo than he needed to.

"Wake up." Dr. Happy brought the back of his hand across Constantine's face in a swift motion, but to no effect. He then reached over and rubbed his knuckles hard into Constantine's sternum, eliciting a wince. Constantine's eyelids started to flutter.

"Answer the question," Dr. Happy said. "Why did you prescribe Blair lithium?"

The response came out as a chortle. "I take it you haven't met her yet."

"I'm starting to lose patience," Dr. Happy said. "Are you telling me that it's just a coincidence that both Blair and you are connected to Casparo?"

Constantine's chin fell hard against his chest and he started to snore.

"Christ," Dr. Happy said. It was time for heroic measures. Dr. Happy walked back to the kitchen and started pulling out drawers until he found a wooden cooking spoon. He returned to Constantine's side and grabbed one of his hands, extending the index finger. Dr. Happy placed the spoon sideways at the fingernail bed, using it as a fulcrum as he pressed the fingertip backward. Constantine jerked upright in the chair.

"Ow! Shit!" Constantine hollered. "What do you want?"

"Start at the beginning," Dr. Happy said. "How did you meet Blair?"

"At a club." Constantine tried to pull his hand loose but Dr. Happy held the pressure firm. "I thought she was just another party girl looking to score. We went back to my place. But before anything happened, I blacked out. I think she put something in my drink. While I was out, she had searched my home. She found some things that I...that I would rather stay private."

"She blackmailed you?" Dr. Happy wondered what Guy would think if he were there, hearing this from the horse's mouth. "What did she ask for?"

"She wanted me to tell her about my deal with Casparo. So I told her that we were planning to...enhance Cam Del Rio. Our test patient. But that he was just the beginning. We had something bigger in mind."

"You're talking about drug dealing," Dr. Happy said. "But not narcotics. You're introducing steroids to professional baseball. You *are* looking to turn the ball club into the East German women's swim team. But instead of winning gold medals, they'll be winning pennants."

"If they want to," Constantine said. "But I think Casparo is more concerned about them covering the spread."

"You told all of this to Blair?"

"Yes. Ow." Constantine pursed his lips. "Can you stop doing that to my finger?"

Dr. Happy reluctantly relaxed the pressure on the wooden spoon. "Why did she want to know?"

"I don't know. I didn't ask. She was very direct with her threat."

Dr. Happy took a step backward and inspected Constantine's face, wondering if he was starting to sober up and just fucking with him. "You sound afraid of her."

"Terrified," Constantine said. There was an earnestness to his voice, like he was trying to get something off his chest. "There's something very wrong with her. All that crazy she shows on the surface is just the first layer of the onion. Underneath I suspect there is something much worse."

Dr. Happy held up the spoon to his mouth. Things were not unraveling the way he had predicted. "How soon after you first met with Casparo did Blair approach you?"

"Not long. Only, I never met with Casparo. I told you the other night, I was approached by one of his associates."

"One of his associates?" Dr. Happy said. "You said this is a gambling angle. Rip Mancuso runs the gambling racket for the syndicate. Is Rip the one who approached you?"

"Yes."

"You never dealt with Casparo directly?"

"I assumed that's how these things are done. You need a

buffer to insulate the boss, right?"

Dr. Happy gripped the spoon with both hands and leaned over to Constantine. "You willingly entered a business arrangement with Rip Mancuso? If I were you, once the Pentothal wears off, I'd pack up shop and head out of town as quickly as possible."

Constantine seemed amused by Dr. Happy's apparent concern. "Why would I be afraid of Rip? He was a perfect gentleman."

"Let me get this straight. Between Rip and Blair, she's the one you're afraid of?"

"Terrified. The word I used was terrified."

"Jesus," Dr. Happy said, dropping the spoon. "I can't wait to meet her."

When Guy woke up, he was the only one occupying the bed. Realizing Blair was gone, he reached over and ran his hand down the imprint she had left in the mattress. The bed sheet was already cold.

Guy stepped out of the bed and walked over to the kitchen where a phone hung from the hall near the sink. He dialed and when the motel clerk answered, Guy asked to be connected to Dr. Happy's room.

"You were supposed to check in last night," Dr. Happy said as soon as he answered the line. "I take it you found Blair."

"Yeah." Guy sighed.

"I found Constantine last night at his other property. And look, there's something I think you should know about Blair."

"She's gone."

"What?"

"She snuck out while I was asleep."

"Your performance must have left something to be desired."

"Possibly." He reflected on Blair's response when he had suggested they just get in his car and take off together, the disappointment on her face.

"Just come back to the motel. I found out some information

that I need to share with you. The idea that Blair's leaving bread crumbs. It may not be that crazy after all."

"Yeah." His eye caught the turntable on the dresser. Something had been left on top of it. "Maybe not."

"Get back here as soon as you can. Make sure you're not followed."

Guy hung up the phone and walked over to the turntable. On top of the dust cover was a thick manila folder with several pieces of lined paper secured inside by the tines of an embedded brad fastener. Guy immediately recognized it as identical to the other folders that were filed away in the Medical Records office at the hospital on Beverly Boulevard. It was a medical chart. Guy picked it up and turned it over, glancing at the seven-digit number on the label, more to double-check than anything.

# CHAPTER 21

"Nigrostriatal dopaminergic neurodegeneration."

They were back at the motel, sitting in the small patio that opened out of the back door of Dr. Happy's first-floor room. Guy sat in a cheap plastic lawn chair, sipping from a paper coffee cup. Dr. Happy occupied the other chair, thumbing through Antonin Casparo's hospital chart with a diligent eye.

"Sounds like the name of a bad punk band," Guy said.

Dr. Happy looked up from the chart. "It means he has Parkinson's disease." His brow wrinkled as he considered his last statement. "Well, not Parkinson's disease exactly. But something like it. Very specific parts of his brain are being progressively damaged, but none of the tests they've done explain why."

"How do they know what parts of his brain are being damaged?"

"By the symptoms," Dr. Happy answered. "According to this, Casparo's showing signs of dementia, with loss of motor control. He isn't able to walk anymore. He's been showing signs of compulsive behavior…"

"How would they notice?" Guy muttered into his coffee cup.

"…Confusion, muscle weakness," Dr. Happy continued.

"Is he dying?"

"He might be," Dr. Happy said. "But the better question is: what exactly did Blair want with Casparo's chart? And why did she give it to you?"

"Maybe she wanted me to know that Casparo's on his way out. That it's safe for me to come back to town. Or at least it will be soon."

"You were already back in town when she gave you the chart, though."

"Ugh," Guy exclaimed, rubbing his palms into his eyelids. "Nothing this girl does ever makes any sense." He grabbed the chart from Dr. Happy and studied the scrawling handwriting on the pages inside. He carefully sounded out the words. "Nigro...striatal...dopaminergic...neuro...degeneration." He tossed the chart to the patio floor. "Still sounds like a foreign language to me. Like Cantonese or Manganese or something."

Dr. Happy frowned as he reached down to pick up the chart. "I think you mean Mandarin," he said. "Or Chinese. Not..." He paused.

"No, I was just joking." Guy shrugged. "I know it's Manga—" He stopped to correct himself. "I know it's Mandarin. That's what I meant."

"Yeah, but you said *manganese*."

"All right," Guy conceded. "I said it wrong. Congratulations, you're smarter than me." He got up and started pacing around the patio. "Does that make you feel better? Jesus, are all doctors this intellectually insecure?"

"No," Dr. Happy interjected. "Shut up for a second." He flipped through the chart. "Manganese." He clapped the folder closed with a confident air. "That's it. That's what Blair wanted you to find out."

"What are you talking about?" Guy asked. "Blair doesn't speak Chinese."

"Stop talking." Dr. Happy sighed. "You ever hear the expression *mad as a hatter*?"

"Like the guy in *Alice in Wonderland*?"

"Sort of. It comes from a real phenomenon," Dr. Happy explained. "In the seventeenth century, the French started using mercury salts to make fur hats. It caught on in England soon after that. The workers who made the hats were kept in small, poorly ventilated rooms. But mercury is toxic, and suddenly mercury poisoning became a common occupational hazard."

"Okay," Guy said. "But Casparo isn't a seventeenth-century French hat maker."

Dr. Happy frowned. "Mercury isn't the only metal that can cause neurotoxicity. You can get sick from manganese poisoning too. Welders, for example. They can be exposed to manganese if it's in the welding fumes. There are well-established reports of it causing brain damage that looks like Parkinson's disease."

"Casparo isn't a welder either," Guy countered.

"They've also seen manganese toxicity in kids who use *methcathinone*," Dr. Happy went on. "MCat. It's a street drug that's popular with the Soviets. It's an amphetamine, like speed. It's usually cooked up by bathroom chemists, and if they use potassium permanganate for the oxidation step of the synthesis, then manganese dioxide gets formed as a byproduct. Hence the manganese poisoning."

"I appreciate the chemistry tutorial," Guy said. "But Casparo doesn't seem the type to cook up his own smack."

"No," Dr. Happy agreed. He got up and paced through the back door into the motel room, holding the chart close to his chest. "But it would be easy enough to slip it to him without him knowing. If you wanted to poison someone in a way that would be virtually untraceable, then MCat would be an ideal agent. MCat can be crushed, so you could put in his food. It can be vaporized, so you could dust his cigarettes with it. It's water soluble, so you could spike his drink with it."

Guy hurried after him. "You think someone's poisoning him."

"Think about it," Dr. Happy said. "Have you actually seen Casparo since you've been back in town?"

Guy shook his head.

"So, how do you know he wants Blair dead?"

Guy considered. "Because Rip keeps saying he does."

"Right," Dr. Happy said. "*Rip.* He's been on a mission to find Blair and put her out of commission. He's been turning the city upside down trying to find her."

"Rip," Guy parroted, trying to keep up with Dr. Happy's train of thought.

"*He's* the one who wants Blair dead," Dr. Happy surmised. "Not Casparo. Think about it."

"Rip wants Blair dead."

"To keep her quiet."

Guy mulled it over. "Because of what she found out about Casparo?"

"Because of what she found out about *Rip*," Dr. Happy corrected. "That Rip has been poisoning Casparo." He dropped the chart on the counter and looked up at Guy. "Rip's trying to slay the king and make a play for the throne."

"But why go through all that trouble?" Guy asked. "Poisoning Casparo the way you're describing must have taken weeks or months. Why wouldn't Rip just shoot him in the back of the head?"

Dr. Happy shook his head. "Politics," he replied. "Before you take out a boss, you need the permission of the other bosses. And if they say no, then you have a target on *your* head. But if Casparo appears to die from an idiopathic neurodegenerative disease…"

"Then Rip has a clear path to succession." Guy exhaled slowly. "Is there a way to prove that Casparo's illness is from poisoning?"

"You test his urine for heavy metals," Dr. Happy answered. "Pretty much any lab can do it. And it's one of the few tests that wasn't done when Casparo was in the hospital."

"Why not?"

"His doctor probably didn't think about it," Dr. Happy answered. "Like you said, Casparo's not a welder or a seventeenth-century French hat maker."

"If we bring this to Casparo," Guy said, "if we turn Rip over to him, he'd see it as us squaring things with him. We'd be free."

"You and me both."

"And Blair," Guy added. "This would be enough for him to let all three of us go. And Blair knows it." Guy picked up the chart from the counter. "She once told me she was going to find leverage with Casparo, something to pry us free with. But I didn't believe her. I lost my nerve and split town. But then she stumbled onto this. Something bigger than she could have imagined."

"So maybe Blair *was* leaving breadcrumbs for you all along?"

"Or she got tired of waiting and decided to try to pull this off herself," Guy said. "Last night, when I mentioned that I was working with you, a doctor, that got her attention. Maybe she didn't leave the chart for me. Maybe she left it for me to give to you. She probably figured it had a clue that Casparo was being poisoned, but she needed a medical professional to look it over for her to be sure."

"She could have had Constantine do it for her. He's scared to death of her. He'd do anything she asks."

"That was probably her plan. I found her in Constantine's condo after all. But when I mentioned you had flipped over on Casparo…"

"She figured leaving the chart for you to give to me was a safer play." Dr. Happy said. "Did she mention anything else?"

"Her stash," Guy said. "She joked that she was just holding it for a friend."

Dr. Happy reached into his coat pocket and pulled out one of Blair's prescription bottles, the one containing the baggie full of white powder. Dr. Happy twisted open the baggie as Guy watched intently. Dr. Happy wet a finger with his tongue, tabbed it into the powder, then brought the finger back to his tongue.

"This isn't cocaine," he said.

"Holy shit." Guy's fingers squeezed the medical chart tightly. "Is it MCat?"

"I can't tell. But we can get it tested."

"And see if it matches what's in Casparo's system?"

"That's correct," Dr. Happy answered. "Blair had all the pieces, and we've got them now."

"Whether she intended for it to go down like this or not, it looks I'm the one who needs to cut the deal with Casparo now. She washed my back. Now I wash hers, and maybe we both stay clean." Guy held the chart up in front of him. "All we have to do is spell it out for Casparo."

"I haven't even mentioned the best part," Dr. Happy said.

Guy just stood there, waiting with bated breath for him to continue.

"It's called chelation therapy," Dr. Happy said. "It pulls the manganese out of the body."

"It might help Casparo?"

Dr. Happy grabbed the chart from Guy and started toward the door. As he hurried out of the motel room, with Guy in close pursuit, he said: "It might cure him."

# CHAPTER 22

When the Jaguar reached the iron gates outside Casparo's house, Guy rolled down the driver's side window and hit the button on the security console.

"Wrong address," a disaffected voice announced from the speaker.

"My name is Guy McCann," Guy said, speaking clearly. "I'm here to see Mr. Casparo."

"Go fuck yourself, pal," the voice deadpanned.

Guy rolled his eyes. "Just tell Casparo that Guy McCann is here to take care of some unfinished business. Trust me, you'll be doing yourself a favor."

The intercom cut out and Guy turned to Dr. Happy. "Bet you twenty bucks we don't get out of this alive."

"Let me see the money," Dr. Happy said.

Guy smiled and reached for his hip pocket.

"Uh-uh," Dr. Happy said. "I don't want Rip's money, I want yours."

Guy handed him his own wallet to inspect. The billfold was devoid of cash.

"You'll have to consider me good for it," Guy said.

"All right," Dr. Happy said, before handing back the wallet. He then nudged Guy's arm, saying: "Check it out."

The gate was opening.

Guy took a deep breath. "Guess this is it," he said slowly, trying to keep his voice from cracking.

"Stop stalling," Dr. Happy ordered. "Let's get this over with."

Guy drove up to the front door of the house where two foot soldiers, dressed in black suits, were waiting for them. One of them leaned over and eyed Guy suspiciously. "Is this him?" he asked the other soldier.

A face that Guy recognized as Mickey's appeared in the window. Mickey smiled widely. "It sure as hell is," he replied. He turned to Guy and laughed. "How's my little playmate doing? You feel like going another couple of rounds, Champ?"

"Not tonight," Guy replied. "I'm still sore from tussling with your mom."

Mickey's smile turned to a sneer. "More like with your dog, you mean," he shot back, looking back at the other foot soldier for validation.

"I'd have to take your word for it," Guy deadpanned. "It is pretty hard to tell the difference between the two."

Mickey's face turned red and he yanked the car door open, pulling Guy out onto the driveway. "What the fuck did you just say?" he barked, throwing Guy up against the side of the Jaguar.

"Hey." Dr. Happy stepped out of the car and walking over to the driver's side, keeping his gaze set on Mickey. "Casparo's expecting us, so he's expecting us in one piece."

Mickey bit down hard on his bottom lip and let go of Guy. The two soldiers escorted Guy and Dr. Happy into the house in silence. They walked to the French doors outside Casparo's office. Mickey and his partner stopped, and they shot Guy an ugly look.

"Go ahead," Mickey prompted.

Guy looked at Dr. Happy, who nodded in return. Guy took a deep breath and opened the doors.

Inside, Casparo sat next to his desk. Guy immediately noticed the change in his appearance. He had lost over twenty pounds of body weight, and the leftover skin hung loosely under his chin.

Guy first thought there was something strange about the way he was sitting until he realized he was in a wheelchair, a dusty gray blanket covering his legs. His face was frozen in an expressionless mask. Next to him stood Anneleise Casparo. She looked at Guy with the same cold air that she carried the night he first saw her.

Without moving his head, Casparo's eyes slowly rose to meet Guy's. In a slow, raspy voice, he spoke: "The *consigliere* returns. And I see you've brought *il dottore*."

Guy and Dr. Happy stood silently at the threshold.

"Please, please," Casparo continued, slowly raising an arm in what was meant to be a welcoming gesture. However, the awkward rigidity of his movements made it seem like someone else was controlling his actions. "Come inside." He took a long, agonizing breath. "Make yourself comfortable."

"You seem surprisingly pleased to see us," Guy said. He and Dr. Happy slowly walked into the room.

Casparo made another effortful arm motion to Mickey, who stepped further back into the hallway and closed the door, leaving the four of them alone in the office. "I am," Casparo replied. "Especially the good doctor. I am especially glad you are here this evening."

"Why is that?" Dr. Happy asked.

"Because I would like you to kill me," Casparo answered.

Guy threw a glance to Dr. Happy. "Compulsive behavior? Confusion?"

Dr. Happy started to nod but Casparo began awkwardly waving his hand again.

"No, no," he replied. "My request is not a symptom of my condition, but rather a reaction toward it." He held a trembling hand out toward Dr. Happy. "I have become a prisoner in my own body, and I am merely asking you to release me."

Dr. Happy addressed Anneleise Casparo. "Is he serious?" he asked.

"Leave her out of this," Casparo said. "I already asked her to do it, but she doesn't have the nerve. I even bought her a gun to do it with." He reached over to the desk and lifted up a pearl-handled, silver-plated .22 snub-nosed revolver. He cradled the gun in his hands and looked down at it affectionately. "This is a weapon worthy of taking my life," Casparo announced. "Small-caliber bullet so that there's no messy exit wound." He looked up at Dr. Happy with his expressionless face. "The rugs in here are Persian," he explained. "Priceless."

"Before we get to that," Guy began, "we need to tell you something. Something about your good friend Rip."

"Oh yes, Rip," Casparo said. "What trouble has the dear boy been getting into this time?"

"He's killing you," Guy answered. "He's been killing you one brain cell at a time. He's the reason you're stuck in that wheelchair right now.

Casparo's jaw dropped open slightly. "What? What nonsense are you peddling here?"

"It's true," Dr. Happy said. "Your condition. Nigrostriatal dopaminergic neurodegeneration. That's what your doctor called it, right? The one who admitted you to the hospital on Beverly Boulevard last month to run tests. He couldn't figure out what's causing your brain to deteriorate but I think I know what it is."

"Are you serious?" Anneleise asked. "Dr. Jennings said he had exhausted every possibility."

"I know." Dr. Happy held up Casparo's medical chart. "I read his notes. He assumed it was caused by something from within. I think it's being caused by something from without. I think it's manganese toxicity." Dr. Happy took a cautious step toward Casparo. "I think Rip has been poisoning you so he can take over the business."

"Nonsense," Casparo replied. "You've come here to try to gain my favor by filling me with false hopes. I've been examined by the best doctors in the world and I'm to believe some charlatan snake oil salesman has solved the puzzle that's left them all stymied?"

"You don't have to believe me," Dr. Happy said. "You can prove I'm wrong with a simple medical test." He pulled Blair's baggie out of his coat pocket and held it up. "And I think this is the poison itself. We got it from an employee of yours named Blair Weston, and we think she stole it from Rip."

"Blair?" Casparo's voice lowered. "Now I'm sure you're lying. You must think I was born yesterday to believe such a conspiracy coming from the likes of the three of you."

Dr. Happy approached the wheelchair, holding out the baggie like an olive branch, placing it on the blanket on Casparo's lap. "You don't have to believe me. Have that tested and find out for yourself."

Casparo's face wrinkled in response. "You're wrong," he retorted.

"But if he's not," Guy began.

"You're wrong!" Casparo repeated.

"But if he's not?" Anneleise Casparo shouted. The three men looked over at her. Her chest was moving up and down rapidly. "If he's not wrong, then what?"

"There might be a cure," Dr. Happy answered. "It's called chelation therapy. It absorbs the manganese and leeches it from your body. It should keep you from getting worse. It might make you better."

Casparo sat silently in his wheelchair.

"If what they're saying is true, we need to get in touch with Dr. Jennings immediately," Anneleise said. Her voice was heavy. "I should call him at once."

"That's a good idea," Dr. Happy said. "He can test for heavy metals in his urine. Testing those against what's in that bag will confirm our suspicions."

"I'll send for him right this minute," Anneleise announced. Guy and Dr. Happy stood still, breathless, as she rushed out of the room.

Once she was gone, Casparo addressed Guy. "And you think Rip is responsible for this?"

"Let me ask you this," Guy replied. "Rip's been running all over LA looking for Blair so he could fit her for a pair of concrete high heels. Did you order the hit on her?"

"No," Casparo answered. "I did not."

"Did you know that Rip approached a doctor named Immanuel Constantine to rig baseball games by giving steroids to players, starting with one named Cam Del Rio?" Dr. Happy asked.

Casparo reacted as if he had been shot full of Novocain. He sat with his lips slightly parted, his eyes betraying a sense of confusion.

"Then that answers your question," Guy said. "Rip's looking to expand his business and he's poisoning you to clear you out of the way. Blair found out and was going to tell you in exchange for her freedom, and now Rip's trying to kill her to keep her from doing that."

Casparo looked at his hands. In one, he held the baggie and the finely cut powder inside. In the other, he held the .22 revolver. "Then I guess I don't need this yet after all." He reached out to place the gun onto his desk, the weapon shaking precariously as he strained to complete the action. He pushed the gun away from him, sliding it toward the other end of the desk.

Guy watched the revolver come to rest and glanced at his watch. He knew it was only a matter of time before Anneleise returned with the doctor, and Guy and Dr. Happy's suspicions would be validated. The smart move would be to keep quiet and let the time pass in silence, but he couldn't help himself. His gaze rose to meet Casparo's and he opened his mouth. "I need to know something."

Casparo sat quietly, waiting for Guy to continue.

"Why me?" Guy asked. "Of all the lawyers in LA whose lives you could have ruined, why did you choose me?"

Casparo's expression didn't change—biologically, it couldn't—but the inflection in his voice suggested he was surprised that Guy had to ask. "Because I knew you would do the job," he replied.

"When I met you, it was clear as day. Your arrogance, your narcissism...you wore it like a badge of honor. You felt so entitled to all the many things life had to offer without feeling any obligation to actually go out and earn them." Casparo took a deep breath and exhaled with a hoarse sigh. "The first time I set eyes on you I knew, I told myself, there is a man who knows how to cheat...who needs to cheat...who doesn't know any other way." He lifted a finger, gnarled and withered, and pointed it at Guy. The hand trembled with fine amplitude as he spoke. "And like all cheaters, I knew you were a coward at heart. I knew I could scare you into servitude. The only problem was, I was too right!" His hand slammed down hard on his lap. "I scared you so good that you ran away like a little child."

"I escaped," Guy snapped. "I regrouped. And I returned. I came back of my own volition and now I'm saving your life."

"My life?" Casparo coughed. "Don't speak to me like I'm a fool. You'd like to think that you are in the lifesaving business. You'd like to think that because of your vocation you are somehow automatically elevated to some superhuman status." He gestured angrily at Dr. Happy. "Both of you! You think of yourselves as do-gooders—superheroes—because of the power your professions bestow on you. But the power to do good does not make you a hero if you only use it for greed...for vanity. You aren't superheroes, the two of you. You are only interested in self-preservation. You aren't here to save me. You're here to save yourselves!" His hands fell to his lap and started tremoring with a fine rhythm. He turned his gaze down toward them, shaking his head slowly. "But you can't be saved. You were spoiled long ago."

"No, we're not the spoiled ones," Guy said. "You are. That's the way I see you. As a spoiled little girl, collecting people like they were dolls, toying with them until you get bored with them and throw them out."

"Ha! There's that arrogance," Casparo spat. "That self-deception. You are the spoiled children. The grown-up version of the rotten ingrates who ran away from responsibility and never learned how to live in a world that requires you to earn something before you obtain it. I am the foster mother, the taker in of stray cats and dogs. I cannot cure your arrogance, but I can redirect it into something useful, something of value."

Guy shook his head. "You used me to keep murderers and rapists out of jail."

"I used you to keep this organization running," Casparo corrected. "And I compensated you handsomely. What did you repay me with? Cowardice and betrayal."

Dr. Happy took a step forward. "Regardless of our past actions or present motivations," he said. "We are all here with a common interest."

"For the time being I must take that on faith," Casparo said. "You believe that my doctor will agree with your diagnosis?"

"I do."

"You'd better be correct," Casparo said. "Because if you came here simply to waste what little time I have left on this Earth, then neither of you is going to leave these premises in one piece."

A silence fell over the room as Guy and Dr. Happy exchanged an anxious glance. After a few moments, Guy saw Anneleise open the French doors and step back into the room.

"The doctor's here," Guy said.

"That was fast..." Dr. Happy began as the three men turned in time to see the doors swing wide open and Rip walk into the room. With one hand, he was holding onto Blair, pinning her wrists together with his grasp. With his other hand he was holding a .38 caliber pistol.

# CHAPTER 23

Rip's entrance initially caused Guy to freeze in his tracks. But when he saw Blair, he instinctively took a step toward her.

"Uh-uh," Rip warned, raising the gun toward Guy.

Guy felt his muscles tense. He didn't take another step, but he didn't back up either. Noticing this, Rip lifted the barrel of the gun to Blair's temple.

"She knows I'll kill her," Rip said. "That's why she's displaying such good behavior." He narrowed his gaze at Guy. "You might consider following her example."

Guy silently stepped back toward the desk, closer to where Dr. Happy was standing.

"Why don't you come right in, Rip?" Dr. Happy said. "I'm just here to make a house call."

"Right," Rip scoffed. "And Michael Kuzak here just showed up to do some pro bono work."

Guy turned to Casparo, who just sat frozen in his chair.

"Suppose he is," Dr. Happy said. "What services did you come here to render tonight?"

"Me?" Rip asked. "I'm the rat exterminator." He turned to Casparo. "Boss, I don't know what these two fucksticks have been selling you, but it's all bullshit. They're tied up with this crazy cunt, who's having delusions of grandeur."

Blair bared her teeth at Rip. "Don't call me that," she

growled from under his grip. "I don't like that word."

"Is that so?" Rip replied. He pushed the muzzle of his .38 harder against her temple and looked back up at Dr. Happy. "The only lead I had was the pictures of this *cunt* dolled up like Scarlett O'Hara at the ballpark that this *cunt* left in her hotel room." Rip tightened his grip on Blair's wrists. "So I took a visit to the ballpark, and found out that a couple of idiots had been sniffing around one of the ballplayers. A ballplayer who just happens to have a personal physician who's a close associate of mine." Rip widened his glare so he was looking at both Guy and Dr. Happy. "Apparently the two idiots said they were doctors and were making some medical inquiries. I found that interesting. So I decided to visit my physician associate, to find out if he knew what these two idiots were up to." He glanced back at Blair. "I didn't find Constantine, but I did find something else."

"Rip," Casparo called. "These two men were just suggesting I get some new medical tests done. Poison testing."

"What poison?" Rip asked. "These two traitors will say anything to save their skins."

"This poison," Casparo answered. He raised up his arm, holding the baggie by the corner so that Rip could see its contents. Rip's pupils oscillated side to side as he watched the snowy white contents rhythmically sway in Casparo's palsied grip.

"Once we test the manganese levels in that against what's in Casparo's blood," Dr. Happy began, breaking Rip's attention, "you're going to have a lot of explaining to do."

"Uh oh," Blair said. Even with the gun barrel pressed against her head she was able to deliver an annoying tone. "Looks like they found my stash."

Rip grit his teeth and shoved Blair away from him. She fell forward violently, just managing to catch herself on the edge of Casparo's desk to keep from falling to the floor. Blair caught her breath and straightened herself before spinning so she was facing Guy. "I told you I was just holding it for a friend."

Guy still hadn't regained his equilibrium since Rip entered

the room. Now that Blair was out of Rip's grip, he felt himself catching up to the situation, but something still didn't add up. "Wait," Guy said. "The ballpark, Constantine's condo. That's how you found Blair." He started to point toward Rip but then thought better of it and opened up his hands in a less threatening gesture. "But how did you know to come here tonight?"

"Yeah, Rip," Dr. Happy added. "How did you know we were here?"

Blair rolled her eyes. "Really, Cagney and Lacey? You two can't even figure that one out?" She shot a dagger stare over toward the corner of the room.

Guy followed her gaze and found himself looking at Anneleise Casparo with a sudden sense of realization. "You didn't leave to call the doctor," he said to her. "You called Rip. You called him and told him we were here."

Casparo's jaw fell open. "Anneleise?" he gasped.

Dr. Happy looked at Rip through narrow eyes. "You weren't doing this alone," he said. "You could have come up with the idea. But to poison him?" He shook his head. "You wouldn't just need access. You'd need to be around him several times a day."

Guy's gaze was still fixed on Casparo's wife. "Anneleise," he said. "That's a German name, right? Would you be from *Ostdeutschland* by chance? I hear that MCat is a big hit with the kids on the *bloc*."

Anneleise didn't respond. Her iron scowl was fixed on Blair.

"Shit," Dr. Happy chimed in. "She could be cooking it herself for all we know. I bet behind the Iron Curtain most the drug dealers are also pimps."

"German efficiency," Guy said, nodding his head.

"Most of the pros probably spend a couple shifts in the kitchen here and there. Is that it?" Dr. Happy raised an eyebrow to Anneleise. "Is that how you picked up the trade?"

"I am not a prostitute," Anneleise snarled back.

"I never met a madam who hadn't started at the bottom and worked her way up," Dr. Happy said.

Anneleise seemed not to hear him, her attention still on Blair. "She is the prostitute." She leveled an accusing finger at Blair. "You worthless ingrate. You are going to pay for this."

"And that's why you wouldn't kill your husband yourself," Guy interjected. "Even if that's what you really wanted to do all along. The gun's registered in your name. And if the DA found out you and Rip were in cahoots, the mercy killing defense goes out the window."

"Anneleise," Casparo continued to stammer. "Why?"

Anneleise walked over to the far wall of the room, putting several feet between herself and her husband. "Because you're disgusting," she answered. "You're not supposed to sleep with the talent. Don't you know what they are for? What they do? To bring that kind of filth into our bed."

"So you figure turnaround is fair play?" Guy asked. "Did you even think about playing the field, or did you just sidle up and present yourself to the closest warm body?"

"Hey," Rip objected.

"So, it's true," Casparo said, speaking to Rip. "My illness is just your cowardly attempt at a coup d'état. How could you betray me like this? I treated you like a son."

"You treated me like an errand boy!" Rip exploded. For the first time his gun wasn't pointed at Blair but instead at Casparo's frail form. "And how dare you call me cowardly! Between the two of us I'm the only one with any balls. I showed you the projections on the steroid racket. You're just too self-righteous to tap into it." He turned to Dr. Happy. "You believe that? The old bastard still remembers the Chicago Black Sox scandal when he was a kid. He said he didn't want that to happen to the game again." Rip gripped his pistol tightly as he addressed Casparo. "The demand's already there, you demented fossil. And since I'll control the supply, I'll know who's juiced and who's not, and that'll make margins on the sports book triple."

"An operation that large," Dr. Happy said. "You'll need more than just Constantine to provide supply and oversee the doping regimens for all the players."

Rip's smiled widened. "That's right, Doctor." He swiveled, bringing the gun level with Dr. Happy's chest. "Constantine's just to cover the East Coast ball clubs. That's where the major markets are anyway. But we'll still need someone to cover the clubs back here. Another quack so desperate to avoid jail time for his medical improprieties that he'll do just about anything. A doc-in-the-box who has learned his lesson from his recent disloyalties and has been scared back into dutiful service."

Dr. Happy gulped. "You have anyone in mind?"

"I've got a list of potentials," Rip answered. "But it's not that long a list."

"Sounds like you have this all figured out," Guy said. He was looking more at Rip's gun that at Rip.

"Yeah," Blair chimed in. "Except the part where the help gets wise to your new business enterprise."

"You have to admit, Rip," Dr. Happy said, "as smart as your game has been, Blair's been one step ahead of you." He looked at Blair. "You read every play like it was color-by-number. I have to know, how did you figure this out?"

"She's spent the last year getting close to Casparo," Guy said. He addressed Blair earnestly. "Right? Since I left town. You found a way to get next to him so you could find leverage. To help us out."

Rip chortled. "To help herself out, Counselor," he corrected. "She might be as crazy as they come, but this slippery little cunt hasn't taken her eyes off the prize since day one." He sneered back toward Guy. "And just so there's what you call full disclosure, from what I hear, it wasn't so much next to him as it was underneath him."

Guy froze, dumbfounded. He said to Blair. "When Anneleise said Casparo was sleeping with the talent, that included you?"

"The other girls told me he liked getting high on his own supply," Blair said. "It seemed like the easiest way to curry favor." Seeing Guy's disappointed expression, she dropped into a mock baritone voice. "Gee, Blair, you slept with an infirmed septuagenarian just to get me off the West Coast mafia's hit list? Thanks!" She then switched to a hyper-feminine tone. "Oh, think nothing of it, Guy! Anything for the fella who skipped town and left me to figure it all out!"

"All right!" Rip shouted. "Enough conversation." He waved his pistol at Guy. "You think I don't know what you're doing? You're pulling the same Oscar routine that you tried to pull in the hotel. Working your jaw and trying to stall, as if the cavalry is going to magically come and rescue you. But for the last time, no one gives a shit about you enough to save your skin." He pointed the gun at Blair and Dr. Happy in turn. "You think these two have been on your team this whole time? They've just been trying to squirm their own way out for themselves. None of this has ever been about you."

Guy's jaw clenched.

Rip released the safety on his pistol. "One positive out of this whole debacle that the cunt stirred up," Rip continued, "I get everyone that I want dead in the same room together." He pointed his gun at Casparo. "The senile has-been." He turned and pointed the gun at Guy. "Trusted counsel." He swiveled and pointed the gun at Blair. "And Pandora's fucking box." He waved the gun back and forth among the three of them. "It's a difficult decision, but I think I have to start with trusted counsel." He rested his gun on Guy. "I've been waiting too long to shoot that fucking look off your fucking face."

"Rip," Blair said.

"Shut up, cunt!" Rip said. He kept his focus on Guy, closing one eye and taking aim.

"For the last time, Rip," Blair said, her voice devoid of emotion. "I don't like that word."

Blair then lifted Anneleise Casparo's pearl-handled Beretta from where Casparo had left it on his desk and pointed it at Rip's chest. Before Rip could react, she squeezed the trigger.

The .22 caliber bullet went wide of Rip's chest and hit him in the shoulder of his gun arm, spinning him around and sending him falling back through the office's French doors. His .38 hit the floor with a thud. Blair shifted the Beretta into her left hand and rushed over to where Rip had been standing. She bent down and picked up Rip's gun with her right hand, then turned and walked over to the corner of the room where Anneleise Casparo stood in stunned silence.

"Catch," Blair said. She tossed the Beretta to Anneleise, who reflexively caught it with both of her hands.

Before Anneleise had time to take her eyes off the .22 in her hands, Blair steadied her stance and squeezed the trigger of Rip's .38 revolver with both hands, firing five bullets into Anneleise Casparo's chest. The first shot sent Anneleise's body flying backward into the leather armchair behind her. Her body lurched with the impact of the following four shots, then her body went limp and motionless.

Blair then pointed the gun at Casparo.

"Are we square?" she asked. Her voice was as steady as her aim.

Casparo didn't hesitate. "Yes."

"All of us?"

"Yes!"

Blair kept the .38 pointed at Casparo. "And you'll tell anyone who asks that those two killed each other, and won't mention a word about the rest of us being in this room tonight?"

Casparo sighed heavily, nodding his head up and down. "You…" he whimpered. "You may go. You may consider your- selves granted severance." His voice deteriorated into a wet sob. "All three of you."

Satisfied, Blair pointed the gun back at Anneleise and squeezed the trigger, putting the final round in her skull.

Guy's stomach flipped and he had to turn away from her corpse to keep the contents of his stomach from rising past the top of his throat. After a few deep breaths, he looked back in time to see Blair leaned over, carefully wrapping the Beretta in

Anneleise's dead hand. As she did so, Guy watched Blair whisper the words: *Consider this my leave notice, you vindictive Eurotrash whore.* Blair then stood up and turned to Guy.

"Hey," she snapped at him. "You paying attention?"

Guy blinked and nodded dumbly. His ears were still ringing from the impact noise.

"Now we just have to plant this one on Rip," she instructed, holding out Rip's gun for Guy to take.

Dr. Happy interjected: "One problem." He motioned toward the French doors.

Rip was gone, only a blood trail remained.

Blair's eyes widened. She handed the gun to Guy. "Take care of this," she instructed. "He couldn't have gotten far."

Guy took the gun with silent obedience and ran out into the hallway. By the time he reached the foyer, Dr. Happy had caught up to him. The two made it out the front entrance in time to find the Jaguar peeling out down the driveway.

"He's stealing our car," Guy shouted. It came out more like a question than a statement. He ran down the drive toward the street until he saw that the car had doubled back and was now accelerating up the driveway, directly at him. Guy squinted, trying to find Rip's face behind the steering wheel as the Jaguar bore down on him. Guy raised Rip's gun and aimed it at the windshield, tensing his jaw muscles and locking his elbows in anticipation of recoil. He squeezed the trigger, but the empty chamber just clicked impotently. Guy looked at the gun in his hand and remembered.

*Oh, that's right,* he had time to think, and then braced himself for impact. But one instant before the Jaguar collided into him, Guy felt himself pushed sideways. He fell harmlessly to the ground as the Jaguar instead hit something else, causing a dull thumping sound across the hood. Guy looked up just in time to see Blair's body tumble down the embankment next to the driveway.

The Jaguar screeched to a halt. For a split-second, nothing

happened. Then, the transmission gears popped as the Jaguar was put into reverse, and Rip tore out of the driveway and onto the street before disappearing into the night.

Guy scrambled to his feet and rushed down the hill, where he found Dr. Happy already kneeling over Blair. "Is she...?"

"Damndest thing I ever saw." Dr. Happy was still surveying her body for signs of trauma. "The foliage broke her fall and the roll down the hill minimized any secondary impact. I think she broke her leg at the hip, but that might be the extent of it. She didn't even lose consciousness."

Guy felt a wave of relief surge through him, erasing the shock and nausea he felt watching the bloodshed inside.

"Don't sugarcoat it, Dr. Kildare," Blair said. She was gripping her left hip with both hands and talking through clenched teeth, but she still had her color. "What's my prognosis?"

"I've seen worse," Dr. Happy told Blair. "But just to be on the safe side, we should get you to a hospital as soon as possible."

She turned to Guy. "Well, then. Don't just stand there looking cute," she instructed him. "Call me an ambulance."

Guy smiled back at her. "You're an ambulance."

# CHAPTER 24

The following few days made for interesting copy for the Los Angeles news media outlets. Guy followed the coverage attentively, grateful not to have his name mentioned in any newspaper articles or evening news segments. The news affiliates and local police alike appeared satisfied that resident industrialist Antonin Casparo had, after discovering his wife of ten years had been poisoning him with homemade narcotics, shot his spouse to death in an act of passion using an unregistered .38 caliber pistol. The nefarious plot of the late Anneleise Casparo had been discovered thanks to the medical acumen of Mr. Casparo's personal physician, Dr. Ezra Jennings of Beverly Hills.

Mr. Casparo had recently been admitted to the hospital under Dr. Jennings's care, during which time urine and blood tests returned positive for the presence of heavy metals that were later determined to be manganese. After hearing the test results, an infirmed but resolute Mr. Casparo searched his wife's personal effects and found large quantities of a white powder that forensic testing later determined was a synthetic amphetamine that contained high concentrations of manganese. Mr. Casparo confronted his wife about the contraband and during the resulting argument, he brandished the .38 pistol and fired six times, fatally wounding her. Several members of the house staff heard the gunshots, including a female employee of Mr. Casparo's who was so frightened by the sound of the gunfire that she ran hysterically out of the house and into the street where she was struck by a passing vehicle.

The driver fled the scene, but fortunately two bystanders happened to be in the vicinity and called emergency medical services and alerted them to the accident. When the ambulance arrived, a contrite Mr. Casparo appeared from his house, having had used all his remaining strength to roll himself outside in his wheelchair. The murder weapon sitting peacefully on his lap, Mr. Casparo alerted the paramedics to the violent act that he had just committed. Authorities declined to disclose the name of the female ear-witness, only stating that she was taken to a local hospital and was in serious but stable condition. The identities of the two bystanders who called the ambulance, thereby saving the life of the female witness, remained unknown as they disappeared from the scene during the confusion that followed Mr. Casparo's confession.

Mr. Casparo was subsequently arrested. However, legal experts predicted that rather than first-degree murder, he would face the much lighter sentence of manslaughter, and was likely to be granted compassionate release following the verdict, given the serious neurological deterioration he suffered at the hands of his deceased wife and the outpouring of sympathy he received from the community.

Fringe radio hosts and disreputable newspapers made unsubstantiated accusations that Mr. Casparo was involved in organized crime and that a larger conspiracy involving second-tier members of the West Coast mafia was at work. These claims were stoked by reports that the bodies of several of Mr. Casparo's employees, including Michael "Mickey" San Gianaro and Robert "Bobby" Bertolina, were found in an empty lot near Mulholland Falls, each with a bullet through the back of the head. However, the LAPD concluded that these killings were a result of a botched robbery attempt and were unrelated to the Casparo incident.

The day after Mickey and Bobby were found, Guy decided

it was safe enough to visit Blair at the hospital on Beverly Boulevard, where she was recovering from a broken hip. Not wanting to take any chances, he decided to enter the hospital from the service entrance. Since Guy had a concussion the last time he had visited the hospital, he had difficulty remembering the route. Therefore, he invited a friend to accompany him and act as his guide. His Sacagawea, you might say.

"Any idea where Rip might have split to?" Dr. Happy asked. They had already come up to the main level from the basement, making a short stop in the lobby, and were walking from the main elevator toward the orthopedic unit. Dr. Happy had been meaning to ask Guy this question for some time, but Guy had seemed very pensive and restless since the night at Casparo's house, so Dr. Happy had avoided the subject. However, once they arrived at the hospital to see Blair, Dr. Happy noticed that Guy seemed all of a sudden much calmer, more resolved.

Guy shook his head and passed the get-well flower bouquet from one hand to the other. "Not one of Casparo's safe houses," he answered. "I imagine it's Rip who is persona non grata right now."

"It might be a good idea to try to track him down," Dr. Happy stated. "He represents a bit of a loose end for us, and we sure represent a loose end for him."

"Rip's got a lot more to fear from Casparo than we do from him," Guy replied. "He's likely to keep a safe distance from here on out."

"You're assuming Rip is capable of following that line of reason," Dr. Happy pointed out. "When it comes to sociopaths, the only thing you can predict is that they will be unpredictable."

"If we did want to look for him, how would you suggest we start?"

"We could call the rental car company," Dr. Happy suggested.

"And tell them what?" Guy asked. "The car's rented in Rip's name." He paused for a moment and then turned to Dr. Happy. "That reminds me, thanks for performing squeegee duty back at the house before the police arrived."

"My last act of service for Antonin Casparo was scrubbing Rip's blood off his hardwood flooring," Dr. Happy said. "If only *that* had been the most degrading experience of my employment with him."

"How did you convince Casparo to cop to killing Anneleise?"

"It was his idea," Dr. Happy said. "I think he wished he had pulled the trigger himself."

The two continued down the hospital corridor toward the nursing station.

"We're here to visit Blair Weston," Guy announced to the receptionist. He held up the dozen withering long-stemmed roses as proof of his quest.

The receptionist's face dropped. "You're not from the press, are you?"

"No," Guy said. "We're immediate family."

"Oh," the receptionist said. Her eyes darted from side to side. "One moment."

Guy and Dr. Happy exchanged suspicious glances as the receptionist scurried down the hall. When she returned, she was accompanied by a young orthopedic resident, his well-developed biceps doing their best to offset his otherwise gawky frame.

"Um, no one told you about Ms. Weston?" he asked right off.

"No," Guy replied. "What about Ms. Weston?"

The resident hesitated for a moment. "First of all," he began, "I understand that the patient has a history of this type of behavior. And I know for a fact she was in her room at six o'clock this morning when the intern rounded on her."

"She *was*?" Guy asked. "Past tense? Where is she now?"

"The surgical incision looked fine," the resident continued. "The repaired femoral neck was well stabilized. She asked to have her foley removed, and the nurse d/c'd it ten minutes later. Nothing was out of the ordinary."

"Hey, Gregg Allman," Guy interrupted. "You're rambling, man."

"Just answer the fucking question," Dr. Happy directed the resident.

The resident sighed. "She eloped earlier this morning."

Guy and Dr. Happy stared silently back at the resident.

"Like I said," the resident explained. "She asked to have her catheter removed, the nurse pulled it, and then when hospitality came to bring her lunch, she was gone."

"She was recovering from hip surgery," Dr. Happy said. "How was she able to leave without anyone noticing?"

The resident just stood there, shoulders raised and palms facing upward. "I don't have an answer for that."

Guy was about to let a few expletives fly, maybe a few punches too, but bottled it up and asked the resident for Blair's room number. When he answered, Guy raced down the hall to the room. Bursting inside he found an empty bed with no sign of Blair. But in a corner of the room, filling the seat of the rubber upholstered patient recliner, Guy found someone else.

"¡El abogado!" Rico the Pimp greeted him. "How nice of you to visit." His eager eyes noticed the bouquet in Guy's hand. "And you brought me flowers. How sweet."

Guy couldn't believe what he was seeing, but the familiar smell of corn chips and gym socks confirmed to Guy that he was not hallucinating. Rico was sitting in the hospital room, flashing a grin that was almost lascivious in its intensity. He was flanked by two *soldados*, whose baggy pants displayed the bulging outlines of concealed firearms.

"What...what are you doing here?" Guy was finally able to ask.

Rico frowned. "What am I doing in Los Angeles? The answer to that should be easy for someone as smart as you are. I am protecting my investment. You are on retainer, are you not? When I found out you left Vegas so shortly after our meeting, after I so graciously took on your debt to Big Sal, I became concerned. So, I asked your associate Miguel if he knew where you might have disappeared to."

"Miguel? You mean Shady Mike?"

"Shithead, yes," Rico answered. "You should take comfort in knowing that the only information he offered was a phone number, and he offered it only after considerable encouragement. He is a big boy with very big bones. They took a long time to break. *Mis amigos* were able to trace the phone number to a woman who lives here in Los Angeles. It was a listed number. Very easy for them to find where she lived."

*Diane.* "What did you do to her?"

"*¿La gordita?*" Rico asked. "Nothing. I am insulted you would ask me that. The way *mis amigos* described her, I could tell that she was of no interest to a man of your tastes. So, she was of no interest to me."

Rico took a fresh cigar from one of his men and lit it, slowly puffing at the end until the tip glowed cherry red. "Then, I found out *la gordita* has a sister who was once a client of yours." He exhaled as he talked, his expression conveying modest satisfaction with the taste of his cigar. "Someone you defended on charges of prostitution. You can see how someone in my line of work would find that interesting."

"Yes," Guy said solemnly. "Yes, I can."

Rico clamped his teeth over his cigar and shifted his considerable weight in the recliner, struggling to find a more comfortable station in the poorly ergonomic piece of hospital furniture. Guy stood in painful silence as he watched the chair strain under Rico's body mass. Once settled, Rico plucked the cigar from his mouth and continued. "So, I asked around about who she worked for, and it turns out the racket she belonged to was under Antonin Casparo's syndicate, and run by Antonin Casparo's wife. But the wife is now dead." He leaned forward and pointed the tip of his cigar to Guy to accentuate the point. "Well, to someone in my line of work, that sounds like what someone in your line of work might call *growth potential.*" Rico fell back into the back of his chair. "Señor Casparo of course is in no position to run that racket himself, with his poor health and legal problems. So,

I arranged a sit down with the other bosses of the syndicate, *los jefes*, the men who are busy deciding what to do about Casparo's rackets now that he is in retirement."

"Bullshit," Guy said. "Those guys keep to their code. There's no way you got yourself into a room with them."

"Why? *¿Porque soy chicano?*" Rico laughed heartily, holding onto the underside of his belly and rocking in his chair. "Or because I have nothing to offer men of such high esteem?" His laughter died down. "Wrong on both counts, *abogado*. While yes, I was born in Mexico, my family is from Colombia. Medellín to be exact. You have heard of it?"

Guy's eyelid twitched involuntarily.

"My cousins back home, they are a bit more ambitious than me. While I am content limiting my business to—how did we put it before, *moral turpitude?*" Rico flashed his nicotine-stained teeth at Guy. "They have done very well for themselves in the export trade. These syndicate men I mentioned, they are very interested in becoming partners in this export trade. Enough so that, despite their code and my heritage, we agreed that if I make sure that this partnership takes place, I would be allowed to take over the prostitution racket, effective immediately. I thought Las Vegas was big time, but out here? This is the real big time." Rico bit down on his cigar and loudly clapped his hands in front of him. "So, that is why I am here in Los Angeles. And that is why you are staying on my retainer, my big time lawyer. To help with my transition from Vegas out here."

"Whatever deal the syndicate made with you, I'm not part of it," Guy said. "Casparo let me go."

"Any agreement you had with Casparo has nothing to do with me." Rico's jovial tone suddenly turned forbidding. "Your debt to Big Sal is now your debt to me. And you will remain in my debt until I say so."

Guy felt a wave of nausea flow through him. "Okay. What does that have to do with Blair? Why are you in this hospital room?"

"Your services aren't the only ones I wish to carry over from Casparo's racket. From what I hear about *tu novia* Blair, she is no common *puta*. Anneleise had her performing more than just blowjobs, my friend." Rico stretched behind him to throw a knowing wink at one of his men. "Blair was her...¿*cómo se dice?*...the knife with the corkscrew and the thing the girls use for their nails, and all that other stuff?"

Rico shot Guy an awkward stare and held it until Guy answered him. "Swiss army knife?" Guy could taste the bile in the back of his throat as he spoke.

"*Gracias*," Rico replied. "A woman of many talents who Anneleise was able to keep in line, because Blair had a little secret that Señora Casparo was able to use against her. And now thanks to *los jefes*, I know that secret, and I plan on using Blair's talents as Anneleise did, and for a very long time. That is why I came to this hospital room, with *mis amigos*. To inform Blair of the new terms of her employment." Rico pointed his cigar to the floor and let the ash drop to the linoleum. "But when I arrived, she had already left. Maybe she knew I was coming. They say *las mujeres* have a sixth sense, am I right? Or maybe she just got bored and decided it was time for her to fly away again."

Guy's head was swimming. He had more questions than he could count, but one bubbled to the surface faster than the others. "What was Blair's secret? What did Anneleise have that Blair was trying to leverage herself out of?"

"Blair never told you?" Rico seemed disappointed in Guy. "The very first job Anneleise put her on, the john got rough with her." Rico took another puff on his cigar. "Blair was supposed to smile and take it like a pro, but for some women that just isn't in their nature, wouldn't you agree? Instead, she got rough back, and before she knew it, she had a dead body on her hands."

"Anneleise covered it up for her?"

Rico nodded. "The dead man has a very powerful family I understand, and from what I hear, they are still looking for closure."

"Who was he?"

"All in good time. For now, you and I have business to discuss. I need you back in Nevada to help settle things out there. Get yourself on the first flight tomorrow morning. One of my men will be waiting for you at the airport in Vegas when you get off the plane. I expect you to be ready to get to work. *¿Entiendes?*"

Rico tossed the cigar butt onto the floor and pushed down on the armrests of his chair with both hands, grunting as he stood up. His men following two steps behind him, Rico headed towards the exit, giving Guy a playful smack on the cheek as he walked past. Guy barely felt it. A few minutes later, Dr. Happy entered the room. He waited patiently for Guy to speak first.

"She's gone again," Guy said after several seconds had passed. His shoulders hung limp, his arms dangling at his sides. "And nothing has changed."

# CHAPTER 25

Guy stepped out of the taxi and walked to the front door of the house in Eagle Rock. He was still numb from his encounter with Rico and didn't even notice the hard surface of the front door under his knuckles when he knocked. Diane answered the door and when she saw Guy, she burst into tears.

"Guy? What are you doing here?" She lunged toward him, attempting to wrap her arms around him.

Guy tried to back away from her. "I just wanted to make sure you were okay. I heard that you had—"

"*I'm* okay?" She cut in. "You look like you haven't slept in a week."

"I'm fine." He was still shell-shocked, his words coming out in fragments. "I just came from the hospital. To visit Blair. But she was gone. They lost her."

"They lost her *what*?"

"They lost *her*," he clarified. "She eloped. It means she left the hospital against medical advice without telling anybody. She just took off without anyone realizing it."

Diane ushered Guy into the living room and sat him down on the couch. Before he realized it, she had handed him a cup of chamomile tea that he had no interest in drinking.

"Why would she leave the hospital like that?" Diane asked. "I hope it wasn't because of what I said to her." Diane's eyes started to well up again. "I visited her yesterday. I was so upset with her about what she's been putting me through with her behavior. She needs to start taking care of herself. I told her that when she was discharged, I wanted her to stay here until she got herself back on her feet." A hand flew to her breast. "You don't think that's why she took off like that, do you?"

"There were probably other factors at play," Guy answered. He glanced around the living room. The Jesus statues remained proudly on display. "Probably."

"She was always unstable, you know," Diane continued. "Our parents had trouble dealing with it. They were very strict, that was their way. I took to it. I enjoyed the structure, the comfort of knowing the path. Blair on the other hand..."

"Blair liked to draw outside the lines."

"Blair never saw the lines," Diane corrected. "She got herself in trouble without even knowing why. Our father would punish her. He was very different with her than with me." Diane's voice started to falter. "She never told me exactly what he did...and I never asked."

Guy let the words hang in the air, not knowing how to respond. He was surprised to find himself drinking from the tea cup Diane had given him, and even more surprised to find that it helped somewhat. The feeling was starting to return to his fingertips.

Diane dabbed at her eyes. "But enough about all that. I'm just glad that you're okay. Some friends of yours stopped by the other day."

"Yeah, I heard about that. I'm sorry. I hope that wasn't too traumatic for you."

"Traumatic?" Diane asked. "Why? They were perfect gentlemen."

"They were?"

"Oh sure, they seemed a bit...surly at first. And very concerned about you. But once I told them that you were okay, just in town for a few days to check up on Blair, they warmed right up."

"Yeah. I'm sure they did." Guy went ahead and took another sip of tea. "That reminds me. I need to call someone. Can I use your phone?"

Diane pointed to the kitchen. Guy made his way inside and picked the receiver off the extension mounted on the kitchen wall.

"Hello," came Shady Mike's voice over the line. "Who's this?"

"It's Guy."

"Hey, 213!" Shady Mike's voice grew excited.

"I thought I told you to forget that area code," Guy said. "Instead you gave it up to Rico the Pimp!"

"Hey, I kept my mouth shut when he said he was going to break my arm," Shady Mike said. "I figured I could spend a month in a cast for a friend. But then he said he was going to break my other arm. How am I supposed to wipe my ass with two broken arms?"

"If I ever see you again, you're going to find out."

"Come on, don't be like that. Rico gave me his word it wasn't going to be a hit job. He said he just wanted to protect his investment."

"Why would you take the word of someone named Rico the Pimp?"

"You're the only one who calls him that!"

Guy sighed. "Lucky for you, he was telling the truth. Now listen, I need to you to set up a meeting with Big Sal. I need to see if he can settle things with Rico for me."

"I can set up the meeting," Shady Mike said. "But I wouldn't get your hopes up. Rico's got Sal spooked."

"What? Sal's a made guy."

"Yeah, but Rico's juiced in with the Colombians. The rules don't mean anything to those guys. As far as anyone out here's concerned, Rico's untouchable."

"Wait." Guy paused to switch the receiver to the other ear. "You knew that Rico's connected to a goddamn cocaine cartel?"

"It's not like he keeps it a secret," Shady Mike said. "Besides, what does it matter to you? All of a sudden you're on the side of angels or something?"

"Anything else about my new employer you've been holding back from me?"

"That whole Spanglish thing he does when he talks," Shady Mike said. "It's just an act. But I figured you guessed that already."

"Un-fucking-believable."

Guy hung up the phone and looked about Diane's house, taking in the New Testament décor. Every portrait, carving, figurine, and snow globe advertised the promise of redemption, but Guy's heart weighed heavy in his chest. *On the side of angels?*

"Who am I kidding?" he said out loud to himself.

"Look at it this way," Dr. Happy said. "This is a vertical career move. You now represent *international* clientele."

They were sitting across from each other at an airport bar at LAX, a one-way ticket to Las Vegas-McCarran International in Guy's pocket. Guy had already finished his scotch and was wondering if it was such a great idea if he ordered another.

"Goddamn Rico the Pimp," Guy said. "I really underestimated that fat fuck."

"I know what it's like to think you're the smartest guy in the room," Dr. Happy offered. "You take it for granted and it gets you in trouble every once and a while."

"Given the events of the last week, you can consider your point well taken."

"Consider this, with Rip still at large, Rico is probably your best protection against disembowelment. At least there's that."

"*If* he's still at large. You'd think that a shoulder wound like the one Rip took would cause someone to bleed out before they made it to the nearest hospital."

"That only applies to human beings," Dr. Happy said. "I'm not taking any chances, and neither should you."

Guy swirled the dregs at the bottom of his glass with a morose expression on his face. "Well, at least you earned your independence out of all this. So, what does that mean for you, now that you can do whatever you want?"

"After I see you off, I need to head back to town to settle a couple things. But then I'm hitting the road myself." Dr. Happy took a sip of seltzer water from his glass and cleared his throat. "Hide out-of-state until the statute of limitations on my unlicensed medical work expires."

"That's three years," Guy said. "Just for any civil action. If the state decides to go after you on criminal charges, that's a whole other story."

"Just as well. I don't tan anyway. What about you?"

"What choice do I have?" Guy asked. "I've got to make a good impression with my new boss. Who knows? Maybe Rico and the syndicate boys won't be able to play nice together and they'll end up killing each other. I guess for now I'll just have to keep my nose clean."

"That's the smart thing to do. But what are you really going to do?"

Guy didn't answer.

Dr. Happy frowned. "Running off to find Blair isn't going to solve any of your problems. You thought it would before, but here you are right back in the same mess. And if Rico is looking for her too, even if you do find her, he's just as likely to find you as well."

Guy's hands fell from his rocks glass to his sides. "Looking for Blair gave me a sense of purpose for the first time in a long time. I can't explain why I feel this way, but I know that her and I have a connection." His hands came together in his lap, his fingers interlocking almost like he was in prayer. "Now that I know what Anneleise had on her, I feel like there's some way that I can help her and we can finally be together for real. Without any of this other bullshit pulling us apart."

"I hear you say these things, but the reality is that you hardly know her at all. There is a very high probability that Blair is a dangerous sociopath that doesn't care about you any more than she cares about the two people she just put bullets into."

Guy thought back to his last conversation with Diane. "I know her well enough, and I'm willing to take my chances."

Dr. Happy sighed. "I was afraid of that." He reached into his shirt pocket and produced a postcard, tossing it across the table to Guy. "When I went by the motel, the front desk said this had just arrived in the mail. It's addressed to you. I thought about not giving it to you, for your own good. But I guess it's not my place to be so paternalistic, and I just can't take that goddamn lost puppy dog look on your face anymore."

Guy picked up the postcard and squinted at it. The front of the postcard had the words *Greetings From The Big Apple* written in a bright red serif font over a stock photo of Times Square. Guy turned it over. On the back, someone had written with red ink in large cursive letters:

*Call me,*

*Crazy*

"It's not much of a lead," Dr. Happy said.

"It's a start," Guy replied. "If I want her, I'll find her. If she wants me, she'll be found."

Realizing he had lost Guy's attention for good, Dr. Happy sighed. "Well, I have to go." He stood up. "If you're still going to Vegas, I think your gate is just around the corner."

"Right," Guy said. He was still looking at the postcard.

"Right," Dr. Happy said. He sounded unconvinced. "I'll see you on the other side."

Guy snapped out of his state and rose to meet him, extending his arm. "Thanks for being on the level with me."

Dr. Happy reached out and shook his hand. "Thanks for being only a mild pain in my ass."

Guy fell back in his seat and watched Dr. Happy walk off, and in doing so, couldn't help spot the departure board that stood twenty yards down the terminal from where he was sitting. A flight was leaving for LaGuardia in forty-five minutes.

Guy held up his empty rocks glass. Back near the bar, a waitress was announcing a two-for-one drink special.

He checked the departure board again. Just past noon on a Wednesday, hardly a busy travel day. Most of the flights he had watched take off from the bar had been half full at best.

*Your gate is just around the corner.*

Guy closed his eyes and tried to will himself into action. But all he could think about was how far he had fallen and how little he had left to lose.

Guy stood up, the postcard tight in his grip, and headed toward the terminal. He imagined the waitress returning to the table to find the empty rocks glass on top of his unused boarding pass for flight 518 to Las Vegas. She'd twist her lipstick-clad mouth into an irritated scowl and say: *Nice tip, asshole.*

Let her call him whatever she wanted. He was no longer there.

# ACKNOWLEDGMENTS

I started writing this book a long time ago and it never would have seen the light of day had it not been for my wife's not-so-gentle prodding to finally get it out there. So, thanks T. You're the best.

Much appreciation to Chris Rhatigan for his amazing editorial skills and insights. Working with him was a game changer.

Special thanks to Eric Campbell and Lance Wright for giving this book a home, and to those who provided early encouragement for a wannabe writer who had no idea what he was doing.

**CHUCK MARTEN** is a crime novelist living outside New York City. He is also a practicing physician, which is to say that he has plenty of experience cleaning up other people's messes. This is his first novel.

**BOOKS**

On the following pages are a few
more great titles from the
Down & Out Books publishing family.

For a complete list of books and to
sign up for our newsletter,
go to DownAndOutBooks.com.

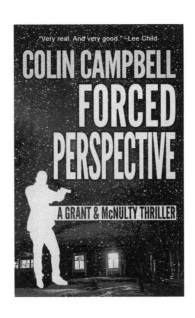

*Forced Perspective*
A Grant & McNulty Thriller
Colin Campbell

Down & Out Books
December 2021
978-1-64396-241-2

Jim Grant enlists Vince McNulty's help to invite criminals to audition as movie extras. The plan is almost derailed when McNulty and Grant protect a girl from an angry biker but the plan is successful. Mostly.

Except the sting is a dry run for the main person Grant wants to arrest; a crime lord movie buff in Loveland, Colorado. A sting that won't be nearly as successful.

*Moonlight Kills*
A Dick Moonlight PI Thriller
Vincent Zandri

Down & Out Books
January 2022
978-1-64396-244-3

When Dick Moonlight PI and his professional impersonator sidekick, Fat Elvis, uncover the head of a decapitated, long blond-haired woman under the floorboards of an under-construction luxury home, they come into contact with a husband-and-wife construction team who also fancy themselves Hollywood filmmakers. Only, it turns out that the filmmakers aren't interested in making romcoms, but instead, snuff films.

With Fat Elvis the perfect candidate for a starring role in their new film, Moonlight is hired by the police to go undercover and expose the operation.

*Razing Stakes*
The De La Cruz Case Files
TG Wolff

Down & Out Books
February 2022
978-1-64396-245-0

Colin McHenry is out for his regular run when an SUV crosses into his path, crushing him. Within hours of the hit-skip, Cleveland Homicide Detective Jesus De La Cruz finds the vehicle in the owner's garage, who's on vacation three time zones away. The suspects read like a list out of a textbook: the jilted fiancée, the jealous coworker, the overlooked subordinate, the dirty client.

Motives, opportunities, and alibis don't point in a single direction. In these mysteries, Cruz has to think laterally, yanking down the curtain to expose the master minding the strings.

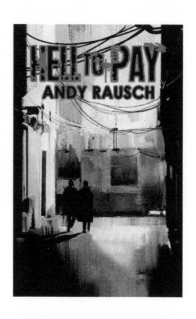

*Hell to Pay*
A Diggy and Stick Crime Novel
Andy Rausch

Down & Out Books
March 2022
978-1-64396-248-1

Dirty ex-cops Robert "Diggy" Diggs and Dwayne "Stick" Figgers have found themselves in a terrible situation. After Kansas city drug lord Benny Cordella discovers that they have wronged him, he devises an insane plan: he's going to force them to commit suicide. This, he believes, will send them to hell, where they will track down Dread Corbin, the man who killed his daughter. Of course, Diggy and Stick don't believe this is possible, but they will soon discover that hell is real.

*Hell to Pay: Diggy and Stick Book One* is unlike any crime novel you've ever read before. It's dark, dangerous, edgy, and laugh-out-loud hilarious. Buckle up for one hell of a ride!